MY SON, SAINT FRANCIS

A Father's Story

MY SON, SAINT FRANCIS
A Father's Story

BY MARCY HEIDISH

MY SON, SAINT FRANCIS
A Father's Story

Copyright © 2020 by Marcy Heidish

LIBRARY OF CONGRESS CATALOGING-IN-PUBLICATION DATA Heidish, Marcy.

p.cm.
ISBN: 978-0-9905262-9-2
Library of Congress Control Number: 2020941926

Cover: Mary Catherine Kozusko, Art Director at Franciscan Media

D&A (Dolan & Associates) Publisher
"A word fitly written is like an apple of gold...."

Printed in the United States of America ....

First edition

In Memory
of
Regis Duffy, OFM

Pace e Bene

The world is too much with us; late and soon,
Getting and spending, we lay waste our powers....
— William Wordsworth

Make me an instrument of Your peace....
— Anonymous
Attributed to Saint Francis

All my life I have been haunted by God....
— Dorothy Day

CONTENTS

PROLOGUE

The Villain Speaks: Assisi, 1228

I have been dead for about a year,
as you would put it in earthly terms.
I am on leave to move about in time
as I will, to see but never to be seen.

Is this sojourn a penance or a prize?
I cannot say, but wherever I may be,
my state of being (or is it non-being?)
has not been as wretched as I feared.

If that is true of me, Pietro Bernardone,
the wicked father of a canonized saint,
the villain of a story long recounted --
grasp hope in both hands for yourself.

Given my history and my experience,
you, too, may be spared the classic
pit of fire, to suffer in a subtler way,
which I suspect draws near me now.

Imagine me as old, a would-be poet,
rusty, slow, a slotted spoon of a man,
here to review my past with my son,
our two lives, stirred into one brew.

I speak of my boy, my heir, my pride,
misunderstood, misused, disinherited;
hence my reputation as a scoundrel,
but it is no easy thing to rear a saint.

Yes, I flailed him; I know I failed him,
but maybe I had to be the dark spark
on the anvil of his youth to ignite him,
blazing up and out into open rebellion.

ONE

Looking Back

Now I move ahead by looking back.
Footprints I have left appear so random,
scattered, stamped too easily, too fast.
Short the way before me, just a crack
of slimming light from one door, ajar,
showing me at least I've come this far.

Let me not be a mere traveler here,
viewing, doing, yet never quite seeing.
Slowly I've discovered life is paradox:
a stone can grow, death is far but near,
the first will be last, night points to day.
God caught me when I'd lost my way.

I found my child only by losing him
through my vanity, my flag of pride,
though he was hard to comprehend;
wildly joyous, then despairing, grim.
I did not recognize the growing saint.
Signs I noted were, for me, too faint.

Is there an hour left for my redemption?
I will seek some grace within my past
where I read signs for others like me,
hiding weariness we fail to mention.
My son's tracks may crumble like cake.
I will retrace his steps for his own sake.

Look for Him Here

Older than these salt-white slabs of stone,
bolder than the winter winds that scold them,
all of our enduring hills are charged with life,
given by the One who spoke them into being.

So my son told us here and others far beyond,
but that was later, after he went his own way.
Or else, as he believed, that way was God's.
I was slow to understand my own son's mind.

As a child, he fell in love a thousand times
with the rhythmic tides of sea-green grasses,
with birds' angelic wings and monkish chants.
All creation revealed the hand of the Creator.

Assisi's landscape shaped my boy forever
more than I did, more than home or mother.
He saw natural holiness in every living thing:
vineyards, hills, larks, tawny fields, blue rain.

Even from the great height of Mount Subasio,
he saw this gray stone town as sacred space:
the stones from God, worked by human hands:
walls, arches, streets --- all for the Lord's glory.

The business of fabric, my trade and pride,
hung like a silent cloud above my son's head.
As he grew up, I thought, that would change.
How wrong I was and have myself to blame.

I see this as I hover here, counting mistakes.
Insight was an uninvited guest, come too late.
Wine was gone; table cleared, no more bread.
So welcome wisdom now, before you're dead.

My Son, My Mirror

Before he was Francis he was Francesco,
my name for him, soon borrowed by all.
Francesco, my apprentice in our business:
purveyors of fine French fabric for the rich.

Dangerous it is to love a child too much,
to mold him and mistake him for yourself.
I did not know this then, as we galloped
to festivals, to fairs, to nobles' mansions.

I saw the years ahead as bolts of brocade,
unspoiled, unspooling there before my feet.
My son, I thought, would give up his wishes
for knighthood to serve the greatest of lords.

How could we have known which lord --
invisible yet near, unexpected yet right,
unpredictable but more powerful than any,
the master soon to rule Francesco's life?

Maybe if I'd been a better sort of father
my son and I would never have parted.
But he was chosen for another territory,
one we did not glimpse or even imagine.

Events balanced on the cusp of change,
but which of us can predict the shifts
that alter our common horizon lines,
the webbing streets, the angle of light?

Only from eternity, as I hover here,
can I detect the slope that is a slide,
the poetry I quit, the cloth I cut to fit,
the signs of changes I most feared.

Colors

It wasn't supposed to turn out like this.
Do you mutter those words to yourself?
I had the future of my son planned out,
rolled up, pinned, wrapped and stored,
securely as I keep my finest of fabrics.

As a boy, he came with me to markets,
those great ones in Champagne, Paris,
across the continent and to Amsterdam.
There our wares were shown and sold,
spread on tables long as village streets.

Silks shimmered like sun-struck steel,
but the fabrics did not interest my son:
material the hues of blood and brandy,
silver and cerise and the purest gold.
It was only Nature's colors he adored.

At home, Francesco ran in meadows,
singing, grabbing handfuls of flowers,
warbling words he had just heard --
puce, plum, turquoise, ruby, cerulean --
jubilant, taking bouquets to the church.

He had a good eye, it seemed to me,
a sense of what is rich and splendid,
what is too dreary to buy or to sell.
This was my prayer on every jaunt:
my son would one day be my partner.

I marked his path with a steady hand,
just as I marked linens with my chalk.
But chalk wears down, chips, breaks;
my path, I see now, fits my mistakes.

Pietro Recalls His Child

I wonder if Francesco recalls
lying on his back all afternoon
in the green of sleeping fields,
where he watched the clouds;
how they moved and swayed
as if to music they could hear,
casting hand-shaped shadows
over him and Lake Trasimeno.

The nearby road was a scribble,
an inked sentence in some book
he could not yet begin to read.
But Francesco favored clouds,
glowing at their farthest edges
as if God waited behind them.
Faces, too, he read them well;
fine, that gift, for a merchant.

My son could leap out of himself
and into another person's world,
to offer a soul *"peace and good,"*
as neighbors bring fresh bread.
But all to him were neighbors,
except one beggar he recalled,
and, of course, hideous lepers;
he flinched at the sight of them.

Francesco, a dreamer, watching
the sun-buttered cypress trees,
listened to their sap run, he said.
Sensitive was he to what he saw,
his spirit delicate as a thin linen,
unready for warfare, yet to come.
First he must grow rowdy, wild,
a young man who grabbed life.

Pietro's Confession

Sometimes I wondered about Angelo,
not mine, child of Pica's first marriage.
Silent, sneering, he was the first to go,
with his fancy airs, his haughty carriage.

Francesco was born as a great surprise.
He went on to surprise us ever since.
He had my face, my pepper-black eyes.
To me he was a long-awaited prince.

Angelo's being seemed an intrusion;
An older lad, he left us on a whim.
I could not love another man's son.
It was not hard for me to forget him.

Two different boys; one was my own,
flesh of my flesh and bone of my bone.

Comrade

"Stars!" Francesco laughed,
a wide laugh, an open door.
He filled friends' open palms
with a flashing spill of coins:
"Stars enough for everyone."

I still see his eyes, lit wicks,
above his funneled hands,
steadier than any barber's,
as if he gave his own money
--- not my gain, my earnings.
"A gift, not theft, so smile,"
Francesco had ordered them.

His family's shop was theirs
tonight: they, his comrades,
were his kin, or so he said.
They called him "*Il Maestro,*"
this master of the starlight,
roistering down the lanes
to bars, barmaids, to wine,
to all the young men craved.

Jostling, crowing, hooting:
These boys had one mouth
to cheer Francesco's leap
upon a table, singing to all,
to the rafters and rooftops.
Police dunked him, drunk,
into a fountain, but my son,
dunked again, rose singing.
This is how I saw him then:
nightly master of his band,
bawdy brother of the stars.

Warrior

Bored with nightly revels, then,
Francesco sighted higher stars:
the honor of a famous warrior.
He would be a hero, that was it;
his sword would split the sky
as he fought to defend Assisi.

My son was brave in skirmishes,
but as a sudden prisoner of war
I saw a darkness fall around him.
Winter dusk where he was now:
in a damp dim cellar, he endured
a stink of sweat, piss, rats, blood.

I saw Francesco, a bag of bones,
war's horrors widening his eyes.
And he, dead silent, just staring
at someone's blood on his sleeve;
he watched that stain disappear
each night, melting in the dark.

A bout of fever; still no words.
Close I watched him in the days
he marked off on the moldy wall.
When I ransomed him at last,
he wore his blood-stain home,
as if it was a sign, an emblem.

For months my son lay brooding,
quivering with fevers and sweats,
until he recovered, strong enough
to roam the hills and meadows.
Pacing, praying, plotting there,
he brewed yet another scheme.

Song of the Knight

I do not demean the quest for glory.
Young men crave it more than a true love.
They seek their place in a heroic story;
the flash and dash of it invades their blood.

So did my son now yearn to be a knight.
From the dark sky he would cut out the moon
to hammer it into a suit of steely light.
Such armor would be his choice of costume.

But some suits may not always suit a man,
as it happened in Francesco's attempt.
On his way, he was warned against the plan.
He turned back then, listening, obedient.

That was when my son gave up this quest.
Glory, for its own sake, meant emptiness.

Why?

Why was he back?
At first, no words.
Fever yet again.
Then he spoke.
He had heard it:
God's own Voice,
commanding him,
"Go back, child.
Serve the master."
What did it mean?
We did not know.
God or delirium?
What a choice.
"Delirium," I said.
My son recovered,
roamed the hills,
waiting to be told
what action to take.
Silence. Nothing.
Jeered at, pelted,
called a coward,
he walked Assisi's
hard gray streets.
My boy: a disgrace,
to me, to his family.
I was furious, I admit.
Expensive armor --
all gone to waste.
Shamed, an outcast,
blind to colors now,
he only wandered,
trying to discover
what he was to be.
He did not ask me.

Pietro's Questions

I heard my son, home at night,
pacing up and down our floors,
as if still roaming out of doors.
Dark our house, but not his loft,
spreading skirts of candle-light
around his bed, his low table.

There, a grove of quiet things:
inkpot, quills, a wild lily's stalk.
Below, his old life, beckoning,
braided notes of street music,
a song, a gittern: troubadours.
Tempting him? Not anymore.

Did war and prison haunt him
as he sank into sleep's waters
where he could find a current
to bear him to a newer place,
past the chains of confusion,
past questions without replies?

Now, too late, I wish I'd gone
to ask if he might want to talk,
but then I could only expect
his face shutting like a book.
Wrong I was, I see too well,
but I felt mutiny in the wind.

My house was a trap to him
I sensed, and I, too worldly
to grasp spiritual yearnings.
I was just business-minded,
he thought, only a bull to flee.
He never saw the love in me.

What Was He Thinking?

Francesco's landscape: gray.
Distant: yesterday's comrades.
He, the king of cheer no more,
the bearer of good times for all,
even called a coward by some.

Old ways, old friends, old revels
looked faded, meaningless now.
There must be more than this?
Francesco sensed God's reach
but what could God want of him?

My son walked, thinking, alone,
like those he'd once shunned:
the beggars, the lepers, the poor.
In their faces he suddenly saw
God's blessing --- not a curse.

My own life's success was a sign
of my favored state in God's eyes.
So I had always taught Francesco
who realized, long before I did --
my measuring rod was all wrong.

I wondered, did he blame me?
Without leave, he went to Rome,
switched clothes with a beggar,
flung away his handful of coins.
After that, everything changed.

Our family's life was overthrown.
I see our house flip upside down,
its floors, tables, chairs in the air,
the front door above in the skies.

A Pilgrim Returns

Left foot, right foot on a dusty path,
trees whispering among themselves,
as he had walked on, staff in hand.
He didn't mind trudging those miles,
he told me after Francesco had returned.

As usual, I said the wrong words,
demanding where his money went;
why change clothes with a stranger?
What on earth had happened to him,
my troubled and truant son and heir?

Did he go to Rome just to escape
from home, town, from disgrace?
No. Francesco had prayed to God
as he took on a newly humble life,
waiting on the Lord's will for him.

Now I was frightened for my boy.
Francesco swung, here to there,
too fast, too freely, too suddenly.
Crazy actions, crazy resolutions.
Was he insane, as people said?

I burst out into our quiet olive grove
to shout, to curse, to calm my spirit,
lest I be called a name I did not like:
a "bully," my son once labeled me.
Deep breaths now. Almost dawn.

When I came back, he was gone.

Troubles

You plant a tree,
even a small one,
say it grows pears,
golden in the sun.
You feed the roots,
you prune the growth,
you watch for snow --
that first year, you do.
The branches reach,
the juiced fruit forms,
so you forget to fear
frost, snow, rot, wind.
That's when it comes,
one of them, all of them,
so you worry, wondering
if the damage can mend;
always there is damage.

When I found Francesco
I thought of my pear tree.
I can see him even now,
sleeping on rancid straw,
again at San Damiano,
home now, my son said.
"*Come back,*" I begged him.
Could this breach mend?
As a young war prisoner
he had been just like this.
Here he sank once again,
at twenty-five and in tears,
pleading to be left alone.
Vowing a return, I went;
the two of us, weeping.
Always there is damage.

A Call

To all of you who cannot understand your children:
Down the rolling centuries you march, a multitude,

bewildered, blamed and blaming, bruised and baffled,
writhing as you wrestle with the past, unable to let go.

You prick yourselves with questions never answered:
What did I do wrong? When was that wrong turn?

There is, of course, no response, not even a whisper,
but you, defensive in your grief, finger grains of hope.

Your faces are smooth, no one can see inside you,
but your innards are rough and sore as blistered skin.

Who even sympathizes with your disappointed lives?
Are you faulted in secret for the way it all came out?

You ask yourselves how to restore what has been lost.
Nothing new presets itself; your children are far away.

In silence parents can be orphaned by their offspring.
Who, among the lucky, comprehends this tragedy?

Who understands you do not sink into self-pity just
because your anguish has turned darker?

Who knows your fitful sleep, your rage, your rue?
I do. I, Pietro Bernadone of Assisi, stand with you.

The Cave

Deep earthen womb it was,
one of our *carceri,* the cave
where Francesco fled next,
afraid I would force him to
quit San Damiano's Church;
perhaps to punish him, hard.
It was weeks before I knew
where our son went to hide,
starving, dirty, hair matted;
a skeleton in a man's skin.

This my boy, this my heir.
How to trust him again?
Could I ever rely on him?
What of us, our business,
the Bernardone reputation?
When Francesco emerged,
he looked so wild, so odd,
people threw mud at him
as we went through town.
Humiliated? Yes. I was.

He looked like a beggar,
squinting in the sunlight,
not glancing left nor right.
In our house, food, a bath,
a bed, a decent roof --
done, I thought. Done.
My wife thought not yet.
Again, she saw clearly.
Early the next morning,
my son joined new friends,
unknown to me just then,
but not unknown for long.

Embrace

When I saw my son among the lepers,
crossing lines that no one ever crossed,
I tried to think I had imagined that scene.
In a field at noon I spied them, I swear it.
Later, the boy said that by God's mercy,
what was bitter had turned sweet to him.

No excuses. No parent should see this:
your child with a walking corpse, ragged,
balancing two baskets of donated food;
one hand, marred, on Francesco's arm.
The leper was dazed with sudden wonder
at the sunrise of a smile on my boy's face.

He threw his head back as calves will do,
giving a big cry of juicy joy, "*MooMoo.*"
Not only had he lost his terror of lepers;
My son looked as if he had fallen in love.
I never witnessed such tenderness before,
not soft but passionate, this strange mercy.

A farmer who caught the two men together
told the others told the carter told the maid
told the butcher told the herder of swine
and by dusk all Assisi had heard the news:
Certainly, they said, Francesco was mad.
As if our family needed one more scandal.

But that kiss was the hinge of my son's life.
He sang as he went back to San Damiano.
At last, I understood what had happened:
Francesco saw himself in that leper's face,
and I believe he also saw the Crucified Christ:
an outcast Himself, at the end, on the Cross.

Keep Away

A leper camp was Hell in a cave.
Our hills held dens of disease.
Every town had caves, *carceri.*
Some of them sheltered outcasts,
built up by the lepers themselves.

They made my stomach turn over,
these twisted creatures in rags,
huddling over their bracken fires."
Keep Away," children were taught;
they did and Francesco did, too.

Why would he now seek them out?
With the rest, he had feared them--
and I must ask, which of us didn't?
Their bells, by law, warned us away.
Surely such outcasts were cursed.

My son had come to think differently.
Jesus went out to the lepers, he said.
Francesco washed them, fed them,
brought them fresh burlap and canes.
We expected his death, but he thrived.

Of all the needy in our town and others,
why had Francesco chosen the worst?
The stench of the shamed and shunned
came over to me like a sickening mist.
Francesco would quit; no need for spite.

I saw his face, radiant as a full moon,
eyes like distant stars, skin smooth.
In this adopted family, Assisi's lepers,
God's children had no boundaries.

The Commission

I watched him then,
this frail young man,
crouched in prayer
on the broken floor
of his dwelling place:
again, San Damiano.

The church slept on,
as its walls crumbled
like stale dry bread.
Francesco, settled in,
was safe, that day,
from a violent storm.

He saw the Crucifix,
life-sized the figure,
gentle the holy face,
flickering, flaring up,
fingered by lightning.
It seemed to speak:

"*Go now and rebuild
My Church; you see
it is falling into ruin.*"
Again, the command.
My son leaped high,
weeping his thanks.

God was with him;
finally the boy knew
what he was to do:
Serve his Master --
not on battlefields
but now and here.

Raid

When Francesco stole my storeroom's stock
and sold it on the sly, just around the bend,
I was away or it would not have happened.

My wife insisted that our son had "borrowed."
I called the raid "thievery," there and then.
A flame-like rage makes me see this again.

"Why?" I shouted. "Why would he rob me?"
To rebuild a ruined church, or so he said;
he had a call from God and went ahead.

Enraged, I chained up my son in the cellar.
This confession stings now, but at the time
I took this way to jolt him into his right mind.

I remember how he bit his lip as I struck him;
when I bound him up, putting him to shame.
As this tale is told, I am given all the blame.

No one says how my hands shook, and I wept.
It sickened me to treat him so, but I was wild.
I did not know how else to tame a willful child.

Perhaps you know; perhaps you've lost control.
Francesco did not realize, nor did he understand:
It was love and fear for him that drove me mad.

I would teach my boy about life's consequences:
A legal judgment, returned goods, cash, fees....
Plans flew to my mind as crows take to a tree.

Would I disgrace my son before our neighbors
or remain disgraced myself in all men's eyes?
I could not sniff the fragrance of a compromise.

The Parting

An old piazza cupped the crowd
as the town waited, as for a duel
or for a sudden public execution.

Their eyesight honed as quills,
their tongues as quick as flies,
Their faces flushed as brides.

No swords, a bloodless battle,
won or lost, soon to be fought
in Assisi's sun-struck square.

With knife-like fingers pointing,
with bets laid, both sides taken,
words chipped the chill of March.

This would be an ancient contest:
father and son locked in combat,
as in jousts of armored knights.

Garish glare of morning; trumpets.
The Bishop, in blue silk I sold him,
entered as we bowed at his feet.

Like an arrow, my voice shot out:
My son must return my property,
all my fabrics and all my monies.

Without a pause, the Bishop agreed.
No response from Francesco --
Suddenly there came a new shock.

Everything Changes

My son laid a purse before me,
then stripped off all his clothes,
set them down and stood naked
as a babe before the entire town.

Windy March enclosed the boy,
who didn't shiver, wasn't chilled.
Feet braced, chin raised higher,
his dark eyes challenged mine.

Time seemed to stop. Sound died.
Birds froze aloft. Trees, skeletal.
Sky, a slate. Sunlight, faded cloth.
Francesco shouted to everyone:

"I called Pietro Bernardone my father.
But from now on I will serve God
and only say 'Our Father in Heaven,'
never 'My father, Pietro Bernardone.' "

The Bishop cloaked him there,
as I, the villain, standing stunned,
sad, enraged, was renounced by
my own child, no longer my heir.

We looked hard at one another.
Hours, so it seemed, we stared.
A steep silence rose between us.
My son and I never spoke again.

TWO

Rage

Once in my mother's kitchen
I saw a cauldron boiling high,
stoked by the flames beneath.
We jerked the pot off in time.

Now I became that boiling pot.
My son left a hat unclaimed;
into our fireplace, I hurled it,
giving it to fingers of flame.

Still the rage leapt within me.
Shamed before the townsfolk,
my honor publicly denounced,
I, Pietro Bernardone, a joke?

My fury grew into a lit torch.
It plumed, rising, by my head.
It smoked, it glowed, it glared
until my wife drew me into bed.

Anger will burn itself to ashes.
That was the fate of my torch.
I blew the ash off into the winds.
Left to me: only soot and scorch.

Meanwhile, on Assisi's streets,
my son was called a "madman."
By instinct I wanted to help him,
but he would never let me near.

I glared; he seemed to wince.
This was where we had come:
silence, like the distant moon,
eclipsed us as father and son.

Spite

In time, that word was my last explanation,
my furious reasoning for what my boy did.
He reversed everything we'd had together:

Instead of lovely damask --- beggars' garb.
Instead of wealthy living --- extreme poverty.
Instead of ease --- begging, labor, masonry.

My son's soft hands were chapped and rough:
laborer's hands for this builder of churches,
for this beggar on the streets, this "madman."

I worked hard to give Francesco the best.
Always I had pleased myself by doing this.
Then I did not see the best was what he had.

Tales about my son shimmered on the air;
magical and mesmerizing tales they were.
He tended plants, the sick, larks, even ants.

I fumed to my wife, "Is he an angel yet?"
Francesco, well I knew, adored Creation,
his a way of adoring the Creator of it all.

And then spite turned into fascination,
a taste for tales of a "new" Francesco.
I watched him from afar, listened to him.

Foolish man that I was, and arrogant,
I admit, I never thought of going to him,
calling for a meeting, a truce ... peace.

But no, I thought, he must come to me. My
stubbornness was an ancient oak.

By the Way

Ah, there he was again,
on the street, in piazzas,
under arches, in a lane,
my son would pass by.
In a small place like this,
it was hard to avoid him;
rare for him to dodge me.

At first, I'll admit, I swore
if I saw my ungrateful boy
I would remember wasted
hopes, plans, money, love.
It hurt to see him ignore
my presence before him.
The worst had happened;
what now could he fear?

I noticed his companion
who did odd jobs in town.
This new job, odd indeed,
as guardian to Francesco,
self-appointed, perhaps.
I don't know, I didn't ask.
As I passed, old Alberto
called down a blessing
on my son and himself
as if to cancel a curse:
mal'occhio, the evil eye.

I cannot find the words
to say how deep it cut:
my own child viewed me
as some kind of demon.
I am no saint, I know it,
but damn it, *not Satan*.

As If It Never Happened

The house seemed larger after my son left.
Our footsteps, echoing through every hall.
It was as if we'd come aboard a ghost ship,
sails sagging without the boy's high spirits.

I remember wandering about the chambers,
but found myself staring at that empty bed.
Did I drive the boy away or did he drive me?
If you'd explained at that time, I'd not agree.

How could everything appear unchanged?
A mirror, stools, a bowl and ewer, emptied.
On a bench, my wife's sewing, half-finished.
A bit of dangling thread, its red diminished.

How the sun slants across the dining table,
melting yellow on the place that's empty now.
I turn away to watch my wife smooth her hair.
We must attend to every small simple chore.

So say the neighbors who have lost a child.
Bring flowers into the house, they advise us.
Poach eggs. Bake bread. Work. And pray.
My wife is at her kneeler many times a day.

As if it never happened? We both demand.
As if it never happened, we are told again.
Opening the drapes will help, so we trust.
After all, no one died. He thrives. And us?

We are haunting his familiar haunts,
but we ourselves remain the haunted.
My wife can't see why he had to leave.
Later on she did; then she only grieved.

Pica, My Wife

She was Venetian glass, winking with wine,
She was French satin, styled for a dance;
a Roman fountain, a Parisian rhyme,
a prayer book, a lute, a song of romance.

She was my wife and Francesco's mother,
Madonna and Mama at the same time.
Pica, a lady of means, like no other:
loyal to her son, yes, whatever his crime.

"No crime," she insisted. "He was called."
She had hoped that boy would be a priest.
My wife was maternal; I was appalled.
Pica was an angel; I was the beast.

At times you can see life's curtain tear.
How do you stitch it for further wear?

Secrets

She went to visit Francesco, I knew.
What mother could resist seeing her son?
Pica took bread, cheese, pears, just a few.
I did not ask, she did not say; it was done.

Now I'm watching them as friend, not foe.
At first, when our child worked on his own,
his mother came often to San Damiano,
talking in whispers as they stood alone.

I can see them; she holds one yellow rose.
He, seating her on one of his white stones;
she, a queen in a ruin, bringing clothes.
No bitterness, no pleas to come home.

Mothers and sons have mysterious bonds,
strands woven inside the womb and beyond.

Dark / Light

It's true, I did look in on my son
...without his awareness of this,
since he did not want me near.
But what parent can just let go?
I do admit to my perverse pride
at the way he got oil for a lamp
in the Church of San Damiano.

By day, the boy visited the sick,
worked on restoring the church,
devoted time to regular prayer,
and lived as a kind of lay hermit;
happy, it seemed, to be all alone,
save for a priest, donating food.
Then, too, he walked in Assisi,
begging funds for building stones.

In town, he noticed the gamblers:
a few men gaming in a doorway.
Wearing his plain penitent's tunic,
he approached the men for cash
but spoke only in fluent French.
Foreign beggars usually do best,
we all knew that; it was often said.
I, shadowed, watched my boy beg.

That night, San Damiano was lit
for the first time in many decades.
The altar's lamp could glow with
costly oil it needed to honor God
and there was also a new bell --
thanks to Assisi's ne'er-do-wells.
At dusk, in time to pray Vespers,
the church was never dark again.

On the Trail

Like a spurned lover, I trailed Francesco,
trying to understand his stunning change.
This was like the troubadours' dramas,
where every word sang new poetic lines.

He had now turned into a brown-robed,
barefoot apparition, a beggar, a prayer,
a servant of the Lord, as he said himself.
He was "God's minstrel," he announced,
singing out to all "peace and good to you."

Crazy? This was not said of him now.
Francesco repented his own past sins;
he did this with boundless enthusiasm.
Some gossip chimed with what I knew.
That boy never did anything by halves.

See this rose bush, fragrant, thorned?
There he threw himself one hot night,
to quell distracting urges of his flesh.
After this painful plunge, he slept well.
In winter, a roll in snow would suffice.

I realized monks did this kind of thing,
some light, some harsh, some ancient.
At least, Francesco's seemed original;
or so I told myself and shook my head.
He fasted, he prayed --- and he sang.

Many said he was too hard on himself.
All I knew was he had found his calling.
I caught that in many a sideways glance,
and in all the stories I kept collecting in
secret pages of my mind on Francesco.

Church of San Damiano

I came back to this old church
where my son's new life began.
Here he learned to renounce me,
claiming God alone as his father.
To be honest, I hated the place.

What was this, what was its magic?
Could a church bewitch a human?
The town was wild with talk of it.
Pazzo, mad, they called my boy.
Was this so? No. Unthinkable.

In the nave, on muted feet, I moved;
no one there, no one I could notice.
My son, out seeking building stones.
Moldy smell of January in this ruin;
July light ribboning through cracks.

Upon my back, I felt a steady gaze.
Turning, I noted the painted Crucifix.
Its eyes seemed to follow me about,
but I am not a fanciful or pious man.
I could not quite dismiss it, though.

Sacred space, this, to Francesco.
Here he felt a change within him
as if he had tasted some new wine;
no old wineskin was my boy, like me.
He was ready, finally, for a miracle.

Something happened here, I knew;
something so powerful, so intense,
it had transformed my son, my boy.
I didn't understand what, why, how.

When?

When I heard certain footfalls in the street,
I'd spring up, throw open the shop's shutters
--- and close them again, often with a smack.
How I cursed, I fumed, I swore; I even wept.

For months I thought my son would return:
the *prodigal* son straggling up the streets;
hair filthy, tunic patched, a penitent at last,
running back to his father's ferocious love.

Was this another mood, a phase, a fancy,
for Francesco, like all the other ones?
When I heard him singing in the streets
I thought he was back to his early ways.

Foolishness. I knew better than that now.
I had translated him into another tongue.
Impulsive, startling, generous: my son.
His spirit shone like a clean copper pot.

This, I think, animals had always sensed,
even the feared wolf he tamed --- and fed.
But this was nothing new, or holy, to me.
That's not what was exceptional about him.

Once I saw Francesco at prayer, in a cave.
He'd retreated there before, but not this way.
In caves he poured himself out like water
and then he knelt, listening, in the Presence.

There he was naked, before the Holy One,
gulping from the source of all his passion,
still stripping himself of old shame, regret,
whittling himself down to serve God better.

A Gift

Like a yolk in an egg,
lodged in Francesco,
was that rarity --- joy.
Everyone sensed it,
everyone wanted it,
everyone wanted him:

My son had this gift,
unseen but palpable
as the skin of a peach.
Before his change and
long after his change,
the joy stayed in him,
and yet it was catching.

Singing to God in town,
preaching at its center,
the man called "lunatic"
now called "luminous,"
--- not at first, not fast.
Like a vineyard in July
Francesco's circle grew.

Why? Why would men,
learned, rich, or plain,
choose a simpler life:
poverty, labor, prayer?
I believe it had to be
the enticing promise
of this new happiness.
A reverent man, not I.
But now I must admit:
The joy inside my son
could only be of God.

Pietro Understands

Try to pack a tree into a trunk.
I, Pietro, in my foolish years
attempted this with my son.
I realized this one June night.

A rare and full and rising moon
hung above the homes of Assisi.
Blooming in the skies, it opened
like one miraculous white rose.

My boy, a poet like me, shouted
as he ran out into all the streets,
announcing this amazing moon,
but the town was already in bed.

Yet miracles must be honored.
He climbed up a church belfry,
high above the sleeping town,
so he could ring the old bells.

Francesco began calling out:
"Guardate — la bella luna."
"Look at the beautiful moon."
"Attenzione — la bella luna."

At the time some folk grumbled,
roused abruptly from their sleep,
fearing Assisi had caught on fire.
But time casts a backward glow.

People still recall that summons
now with pride in our holy man
who first noticed God's gift to us,
awakening the town to share in it.

Wings

What next? God help me, another wild tale;
a new one about that rare one, Francesco.
He had tried preaching to people from town;
excited, even thrilled, they went on talking.
"If you won't listen," my son called to them,
"I'll take the message to my winged friends."
Turning then, he saw a tree full of starlings;
as he started to speak, more birds arrived.
Quiet, attentive, the creatures were silent,
but people babbled about it all over town.

The trouble for me was this: I believed them.
That sounded like my boy, preaching to birds.
I knew it was true; my strange dreams began:
By some miracle I had turned into a starling,
settling my feathers, furling my two wings,
as I heard a little man in a peasant's tunic,
barefoot, hands spread, speaking to us all.
His words sparkled like sun-struck water;
it was a fountain that washed away fear.
On it went and we, entranced, were still.

Abruptly, the dream ended; I woke in my bed.
But I could not forget the dream's fine clarity.
Was I losing my wits, my mind or my sanity?
I set my feet on the floor and shook my head.
The image would not fade; in fact it returned.
Night after night for a week my dreams came:
I saw my son, his face aglow as if by torchlight,
the peace in his eyes spiced with keenest joy.
When the dreams faded, I felt abandoned ---
but a night at the tavern deadened that sting.
For a while, I admit. Only for a short time.

Pietro Tells a Story

When monsters roam the quiet countryside,
they must be slain, of course, by knights:
armored knights on the whitest of horses.
Their weapon, a sword of gleaming steel
to complete their sacred mission --- death.

Dark green forests frame a market town
where the monster prowls in the nights,
harming all who draw near to challenge him:
valued livestock, daring boys and bold men.
The townsfolk pray for help and it arrives.

But how can this short man be a deliverer?
A friar, barefoot, like a beggar in his dress.
No sword, no shining armor, no white horse.
Against grave warnings, the friar only smiles,
entering the forest where the monster waits.

It is a wolf, big as a bear, strong as swine,
growling at the little man approaching him.
Offering his hand, the friar gazes at the wolf.
They watch each other but they do not move
--- until the friar leads the "enemy" to town.

The townspeople still speak of that day,
when one small man tamed the beast,
whom they fed and who attacked no more.
The humble friar returned to his prayers;
the tamed wolf remained, fed, a friend.

If you doubt this, go to Gubbio, in Italy,
where the wolf and the peacemaker met.
You will see a statue of that "monster,"
in time, the town's reminder of charity,
while Francesco went back to Assisi.

New Life

Ah Francesco, you whirled us around,
turned us on our heads and our knees,
dazzied us with your love-songs to God,
your passionate poems to Lady Poverty.

You left us laughing with you in town,
where you sang, reminding everyone:
" 'What you do to the least of these,
my children, then --- you do it to Me.' "

Where did he get the strength to do it?
I spied on his band of men, growing now;
I spied on their hut when they were out:
straw pallets for beds on earthen floors.

They ate bread and grapes and olives,
bread and berries; bread --- and bread.
The townsfolk gave the men hot food.
The rest was dug from fields and woods.

In the streets I saw Francesco preaching,
a broom and a breviary, one in each hand.
He stopped to sweep out dirty churches,
dismayed when holy places were unkempt.

Where did he learn to wield a broom?
Certainly it was not in my own house.
Servants did such work, not owners.
Now the boy saw himself as a servant.

Too late, I solved the puzzle of my son:
Ridding himself of things was freedom.
He had hoped to serve the greatest lord.
Finally, finally, Francesco had found Him.

The Pope and the Pauper

I wish I'd been there. I wish I'd seen it unfold.
Now, through eternity, I view it for the first time:
Vatican City, to our south, and the Papal Court.
This court is hung with silks the colors of dawn,
a serene ship sailing beyond me through time.

And there, boarding this ship is my Francesco,
clad in that plain, patched tunic he always wore,
a brown-gray thing, tied with twine at the waist,
a piebald garment stained by rain, grass, sun.

As the late purveyor of the very finest brocades,
I confess that the sight makes my spirit shudder.
But as the late father of this renowned preacher,
I confess to the pride of the first fruit on a tree.

Before his Papal Audience, still a son to me,
slept with his companions in the lowliest shed.
Francesco wore his choice of humble poverty,
as did the raw disciples of his Master, Jesus.

I wonder now who, in fact, was outfitted in glory.
Francesco needed papal approval for his Order.
Its Rule was compiled from the Gospels' words
but the red-hatted Cardinals were not impressed.

As my son slept that night, the Pope had a dream:
a visionary dream of a man supporting the Church.
His new Order, approved, might increase its growth.
And so it was and so it did and so I rue my absence.

If only I'd accepted my child, if only I'd been loyal,
if only and if only and what if, what if, what if....
A tragedy it is: the dead can't edit their own stories
or I would make great haste indeed to rewrite mine.

Pietro Imagines Francesco Praying

He'd bathe his face in the simple font,
still filled though the church is empty,
always echoing, like a private chapel.
The priest, his friend, stands sentry.

The church, he knows, welcomes him.
He smells flowers, dust, ancient stone
in the only place he'd ever felt at home;
all else was demolished, broken down.

And so he offers murmured prayers;
that sound, for him, a consecration
written on thin air only God can read
sifting down through the generations.

For now, he is where he does belong,
here his harbor, here his only mooring;
here, in gratitude, he would lean over
to lie prostrate on the broken flooring.

He does remember simple joys are holy.
In this place he never was an outcast:
"May I have faith and hope and mercy.
When I grab Your hem it's me You see."

I pray for Plca,
and for Angelo,
and for Leo,
and Lorenzo,
and Bernardo
and Clare,
and Agnes,
and Giles,
and....

What Happened?

"Preach the Gospel at all times...
Use words if necessary."

He looked at his followers and explained:
"Start with what is possible and suddenly
you will find yourself doing the impossible."
Francesco wore a beast-colored tunic ---
ugly enough to make a merchant weep.

Who was this God-smitten man, I thought,
whose face and eyes resembled my own?
Francesco, son of Assisi's richest family,
was once a swatch from the finest of silks.
And me? I had embroidered him myself.
But he was silk no longer, none of mine.

My son was like a cloak of many colors,
seen rightly at a distance of ten paces,
stitched and patched together in private,
lined with pockets of unspoken thoughts,
secret dreams and unexplained desires.
To this part of Francesco, I could not go.

But others were welcomed, newcomers,
old friends, the learned and the simple,
even monied men from the noble classes.
Europe: their parish, its lanes, its markets.
Nightly, my son said, he wrung out his shift,
sunlight and God's love soaked it through.

Like a field red with poppies, it spread:
what Francesco preached, what he did.
Clerics spoke of God's wrath and Hell.
Franciscans told of God's merciful love.
They lived their beliefs, that was clear.
Most preached with words, *if* needed.

Fasts and Feasts

I see a band of feasting men
at midnight, encircling a fire.
They share bread and wine,
passing all from hand-to-hand.
Twelve burnished faces there,
grace pouring like buttermilk.

Had Francesco and his friends
gone back to their old revels?
But no, his small band of friars
sits on the bare earth, no table,
within the mud-and-wattle hut:
their communal dwelling place.

Why midnight feasting now?
For my son, blame and credit,
as usual, swinging to extremes.
He'd designed a penitential fast,
almost total abstinence, it was;
Francesco took it on himself.

"I'm dying!" A cry in the dark.
Francesco, alarmed, awoke.
"Hunger, agony" the next cry.
Lamps lit, Francesco up now,
cooking, feeding every friar
from their stored provisions.

I tell you of this happening
with a parental glint of pride.
After my failed fatherhood,
after my fears for this child,
indulge me in a snip of joy
for a kindly spirit in my boy.

Ring the Bells

As it happens in most vineyards,
growing grapes at first are sour.
Later they turn fuller, riper, sweet.
So it was for Francesco's friars.

My son's mission was ripening fast.
No more hecklers, no thrown stones.
Now my son was called a man of God.
The bursting grapes had sweetened.

As I hover above that shining time,
I think of the great wedding at Cana,
where Jesus turned water into wine.
The winds of excitement stirred us.

And not only Assisi, through Europe,
when Francesco came, bells rang.
The sick were sent to him for healing.
Piazzas filled when my son preached.

And what a preacher he was, at that.
Francesco spoke to the common folk
where they lived, where they labored,
where they walked, wept, wandered.

It was my son's vision of a loving God
that rang out with the towns' best bells.
This little ragged man was full of hope;
contagious, sincere, and unconstrained.

"Repent," he called out, "but rejoice."
God's mercy flowed to all His creatures
if they opened to it, in humility, in faith.
Here, again, water was turned into wine.

A Healing

The girl was dying from ague, so they said.
Her mother begged my son to heal the child.
She was pale as milk; he feared she was dead.
Still she breathed but her heartbeat was wild.

The dim chamber was small, close and airless.
Francesco opened the shutters and prayed.
The face of the child held his awareness.
God had asked this, he need not be afraid.

Under his hand, the girl's breathing changed.
Now she gulped air; her eyelids fluttered.
Francesco knew this was what God arranged.
"Don't go yet," were the first words she uttered.

I tend to believe the child needed fresh air.
I also have come to trust Francesco's prayer.

Crowds

When I saw Francesco come into a town
I liked to think I looked down on a garden.
People's clothes petalled out and around:

Sunflower gold, poppy reds, leaf green,
blue pansies and the purple of primrose.
In the middle, one man in earthy browns.

People cut scraps of cloth from his tunics,
they touched him, they kissed his shadow
as he sat on a low wall, shouting, "Stop!"

He was only a man, a servant, unworthy,
he would say, and they knew he meant it.
Francesco flushed at all that commotion.

It might take away from the brief sermons,
he preached in piazzas, churches, streets.
"Peace be with you," he would always start.

"Repent and rejoice in God's great mercy:"
this ran like a love song in most homilies.
No hecklers now, no jeers, not an insult.

But my son could never manage a crowd.
His friends did and I learned their faces --
Leo, Bernardo, Illuminato. Giles, John.

A garden bloomed at his feet for years,
until the darker times, the challengers,
but those were the sun-dappled days.

Angelo to Pietro

Remember me? I was always ignored.
The name, Francesco, is one I spurn.
My half-brother, lauded by history,
is the prodigal son who never returned.

As the remaining heir I take some joy
in my behavior and my loyalty,
unlike that wild and selfish younger boy
treated by my mother as royalty.

My bitterness is justified, I say.
Even so, I rejoice in my possessions
which that fool tells us to give away.
Why, Father, is he your obsession?

I have the respect of my community
but he steals the show with impunity.

Clare

She was the tallest lily in the garden,
straight and simple and silvery white.
Many gardeners sought to pluck her,
cut her just to own her, enthrone her.

So I have come to think of Clare,
though in life I flat-out hated her.
She, the lily-girl, was a lovely rebel,
quitting her parents to live for God.

My hatred of her was tied to my son,
as he was, in a way, tied up with her.
Clare, at eighteen, heard him preach;
her head whirling, her soul inspired.

Off she went, sneaking out at night,
running then to Francesco's friars.
What a tasty scandal in the making --
but not what you or I might think of it.

Clare longed to follow after my boy,
not as his mistress, not as his wife,
but as a chaste and devout disciple.
A daring woman was this silvery lily.

She took her vows from Francesco
who cut her cascade of yellow hair,
but lodged her in a convent for safety,
until Clare could find another home.

That is the story and I swear to its truth.
My son had drawn the lily from her bed,
a prize no other man could ever claim,
planting a sister Order to Francesco's.

Jealousy

I hated Clare because she brought it back:
the rejection of family, status, and wealth,
a repeat of my own loss and my humiliation
--- but when I saw her everything changed.

She had a strange otherworldly demeanor:
dark eyes, like Francesco's, fixed on God.
Was this catching, these flights from home?
I did not know God, so I did not understand.

Here is what I, fumbling fool, began to grasp:
there are some loves that remain a mystery.
Few can understand most lovers' choices.
Who knows the depth of a marriage vow?

The transplanted white lily flourished indoors,
in prayer, in devotion, and in spiritual counsel.
What a waste, people said. What a shame.
I was not sure and, in honesty, cannot agree.

In the end, I would not keep on hating Clare,
not because of her youth, wealth, or beauty,
not even because my son was her gardener.
It was this: Before that lily, I felt like a weed.

Could I be gardened into something else?
Did I truly want to be more than a weed?
Weediness was familiar and easy for me.
I'd heard too many of my son's sermons.

When I became a merchant to the rich,
I learned elegant and cultivated speech.
A quick ear was mine, I say in humility;
Francesco's words repeated in my mind.

Private Meeting

It might seem to be a lovers' tryst
in a courtyard walled with cypress trees;
one square of light, two figures in a mist;
on their table a single scarlet rose.

They were so at ease with each other,
you might think them pairs for a long time,
these mated souls, not sister or brother;
yet their voices sounded similar chimes.

I wish this scene had been as it appeared
but the couple is watched by chaperones.
Friar and Abbess hold their vows dear.
Francesco and Clare never meet alone.

These closest friends chose sacrifice.
From the beginning they both knew its price.

Pietro, Puzzling

Changes rattled around in me
like coins in a pail or in a pot,
changes uninvited but insistent;
I was not sure I liked them at all.
Early this morning a veil of sun
fell over my wife's sleeping face,
making her a girl again, a bride,

I began to view things differently
but didn't understand what I saw:
a spider's web glittering, still wet,
clinging to a corner of the gate,
and there the hideous spinner,
its bead of a body waiting to be
dashed by my hand as always.

I let the spider be in all her ugliness
to swing and dance around her web.
I can't say why I spared the monster.
Was it a flash of newfound kindness
or some odd admiration for a spider,
weaving her way, clinging to the gate?
Perhaps as I grew older I grew daft.

But there was more to it, I knew.
I had heard my son's preaching
over and over and over again --
repent and rejoice in God's love.
Listen I did, behind a post or tree
where those sermons pinned me;
where I trembled against my will.

Pietro Muses

I wonder if he ever thinks of me.
Not that I care.
I wonder if he ever dreams of me.
Why should I care?
I wonder if he ever has regrets.
Not that I care.
I wonder if he ever prays for me.
Why should I care?
I wonder if he recalls the good.
Not that I care.
I wonder if I'll stop remembering.
As if I cared.
Can you hate someone you love?
As if there's an answer.
Can you love someone you hate?
Why can't I get answers?
As if I care.
As if I cared.
As if I ever cared.

I wonder if he will come back.
Why hope?
I wonder if I will go out to him.
Why try?
I wonder if I was totally wrong.
Too late.
I wonder if the boy was wrong.
What then?
I wonder if we could ever mend.
No chance.

As if I cared.
I did. I do.

Lady Poverty
(With a nod to Dante)

Son of wealth, riches and ease,
he'd become "the little poor man,"
beloved in Assisi and far beyond.
This Lady would be wine and meat
to Francesco if he consumed such.
With her could he serve his Lord.
Poverty, in fact, enriched my son.

Lady Poverty gave Francesco freedom:
a life of simplicity, humility, and peace
could not interfere with God's calling.
I understand now --- again, too late --
after a life filled with my business cares.
Time for prayer? Caring for the lepers?
Not I, prosperous Pietro di Bernardone.

But it was so for Clare, now an abbess.
She had an offer of fertile donated land.
Accept the possession or reject it now?
My son was called to preach a sermon
which would resolve this hard question.
Francesco stood up, sprinkled ashes
on his head and in a circle around him,
said nothing and, in silence, went away.

Crazy, some people murmured again,
but Clare and her nuns understood well.
Francesco reminded them we are dust;
while we live, let us live with simplicity ---
and without rich land as possessions.
My son's unspoken advice was followed.
Preaching, then, had required no words.

Pietro's Premonitions

Shadows falling on my bed.
I remember those from life.
Now, perhaps, I am a shadow.
Perhaps. Not for me to know.

But I recall old dreams I had
at the height of my son's fame.
Dark they were, none of light:
some faceless robber waiting.

A thief of hope, promised fruit,
of blessings and the blessed.
My bedclothes catching sun,
but dimming, draining away.

Then I could but faintly sense
danger coiling in the shadows.
Strange for me, a hearty fellow,
no intimate of sly-eyed dread.

These shadows of the future,
I see now, fell not for myself
but for Francesco, for my own.
My fascination turned to fear.

Like a pickpocket at town fairs,
the fear sneaked up behind me,
in the daylight, beyond dreams.
I shook it off and went to work.

Damn it, I was sorry to be right.
Famed for gifts of peacemaking,
My son was called to a Crusade.
He looked East: to peril, to war.

THREE

The Sea View of Pietro

I imagine my son's voyage
on the frail deck of a ship,
delicate as a woman's palm,
its sails like her blown skirts,
skimming the sea's surface.

This vessel appears to float
surrounded by endless night:
darkness with no boundaries.
Above, the countless eyes of
stars, gazing down forever
through their secret silence.

Once I wanted to be a poet
but business offered to me
a far more lucrative path.
If I'd been a sailor, poetry
might have stayed with me.

My faith would have lasted,
never wavering, I'm certain.
If you doubt God, go to sea;
I can say that with authority.
My son's faith already deep,
went deeper, sailing at night.

What lay ahead of him then?
Would Francesco bring peace,
or conversion, or martyrdom?
He was willing to die for God
but he could not foresee the
disappointment yet to come.

War

There is a stench to battlefields,
a smell of sweat and rotting flesh,
the odor of the dying or the dead,
of ligaments and bones laid bare.
Francesco did not expect this yet
--- until he climbed over corpses,
rendered so by that final Crusade.

From all accounts drifting back to Italy,
the fighting for Egypt's city, Damietta,
was marred by Crusaders' atrocities.
And across those brutal killing fields
Francesco was wading through blood,
to Cardinal Pelagius, the Commander.

I can see him now, this ragged friar,
my son and once my heir, striding fast,
driven to negotiate a truce, then peace.
He tried persuasion, promises, pleas,
but the man in charge was obstinate.
Francesco insisted on risking his life
to seek an encounter with the Sultan.

"You, a martyr? It will help our morale,"
the Commander said, without a smile.
Speaking not a word, Francesco bowed,
turned and, unarmed, with one comrade,
he walked through the relentless heat,
each step leading to the Sultan's camp.

Francesco in Danger

Captured, hands tied, head under a hood,
he sees nothing except his own death.
It is near, it is now, it is calling his name.

He hears soldiers sharpen their swords;
clash of metal, men's voices, their shouts.
He tastes salt, his own sweat on his lips.

A blanket of heat, hard to breathe now,
footsteps close, hands clamp his legs;
he is dragged across scorching sands.

Pitched forward, he lands; sounds halt.
Mouth parched, he can't pray out loud.
Someone there, silencing all the guards,

a gaze is burning new welts into his back.
The hood and robe stripped off him now
--- brutal night has become blinding day.

"Stand on your feet, you spy," a guard spits.
"As-salamu alaykum," gasps Francesco.
"Peace be upon you," he repeats the words.

"Wa-Alaikum Salaam, 'And to you peace,' "
says the Sultan of Egypt, al-Malik al-Kalim.
"He's a holy man, perhaps Sufi, let him in."

Francesco is helped into al-Malik's silk tent.
"My friend, Illuminato," Francesco calls him.
"No spy, like a Sufi as I said." A-Malik smiles.

Only then does Francesco draw a long breath.

A Son's Surprise

My son was not executed as a spy --
he was invited to be the Sultan's guest.
Francesco moved behind enemy lines,
roving there with rare Royal permission,
preaching peace in the face of hatred,
deeper since Constantinople's sack.

No small thing, after such a long war,
a fifth Crusade, fury at the "infidels"
and prolonged rage on the other side.
This was a dark and hopeless picture.
How did a friar and Malek Al-Kamil
come into dialogue on faith and life?

I'd hoped that I, Pietro Bernardone,
had somehow made a contribution
to my son's poise and eloquence.
We had often traveled together—
with me he learned of other lands,
foreign tongues and ways of living.

But in the end, I can claim little credit.
The Sultan saw a devout holy man
in Francesco, comparing him to a Sufi,
whose mysticism the Sultan admired.
But could these leaders stop a war,
layered with generations of hatred?

Francesco's old dream of knighthood
had taken an unpredictable turning.
Now he was a new kind of soldier,
armed with words, faith and prayer,
fighting fighters under a new banner:
Its emblem was the Prince of Peace.

Watch Him Now

The first time you let your child cross a street,
crowded with wagons, horses and strangers,
you scarcely breathe as you watch his feet
taking him across a sea of danger.

So I feel now, as I drift outside time,
watching that scene unfolding once again:
my son crossing over enemy lines,
to preach peace in a camp of armed men.

Francesco, unarmed, walking as he spoke,
held the soldiers' gaze only with his voice.
Its daring sincerity wove him a cloak;
"*Salaam*," or "Peace," was his word of choice.

Its tone, as music can, crossed a divide.
For one afternoon there were no sides.

A Meeting of the Minds

Assisi's friar; an Egyptian king:
A pair so odd it came out even.
Francesco in his patched tunic,
Malek al-Kamil in scarlet silks.

The Sultan, an oak of a man,
wise ruler of many Arab lands,
understood his Sufi mystics;
he saw my son akin to them.

Francesco, a vine of a man,
growing globes of purple fruit,
servant to Western territories,
called all Europe his "parish."

Both were sons of Abraham,
faithful to one Almighty God;
this was not lost on al-Kamil,
nor was it lost on Francesco.

Around them: a sea of sand,
a parched place, strong light,
encircled by glinting swords;
its tent, a fierce sapphire sky.

My son preached to the enemy.
Now he preached to our men,
begging them in God's name
to accept a reasonable truce.

They listened with due respect.
The Cardinal, Pelagius, did not.
All truce terms were disdained.
The king and the friar had lost.

Seeds

Even though Francesco and the Sultan
did not bring about their desired peace,
they stand together in my humble view.
This is how I hope the two will be seen
by others better and brighter than me,
a barrel-chested balding Bernardone,
who speaks wisdom only from eternity.

At a later time, perhaps, these meetings,
like mustard seeds, will turn into trees.
But in my lifetime and in my Francesco's,
there was only the germ, not a sprout.
After weeks in Egypt, the war raged on.
No conversions nor martyrs were made
but a bond, long remembered, formed.

It is my own belief that some people
do the plowing and sowing of seeds,
but others must tend to the nurturing,
as I did with my own needy pear tree.
This takes time, rain, sun, and patience.
My son had virtues like ropes of pearls,
yet patience was never on his strands.

Too soon he fell sick from the climate,
the heat, and worst of all, his defeat.
He was willing to accept martyrdom
for his faith, for his cause, for peace,
but none of these hopes came to be.
God's will be done, Francesco said,
but I know he felt he failed instead.

When It's Always Midnight

Time stops when depression begins
and so it did for my son, Francesco,
on the long voyage home from Egypt.
I knew that he was lost in darkness
even when I didn't see him close:
the slump of his narrow shoulders,
the tilt of his tonsured dark head
answered well my inner questions.

Midnight had always found my son,
after his half-sung exuberant bursts.
Now time had stopped once more;
Francesco counted up his defeats:
He had not stopped the warfare;
What then of his vocation: peace?

What of the Order he'd founded?
It was in turmoil as Francesco left.
He heard reports of the new friars,
talking, complaining, and plotting.
While my son was far from home,
his own Order started to fracture.

It's always midnight in despair.
The darkness seems unending.
Overwhelmed by its tidal force,
Francesco saw all his mistakes
slipping far beyond redemption;
or so my son began to believe.

He was convinced by midnight,
by illness and sheer exhaustion,
by his Order divided in halves.
He thought all that he'd done
was no longer wheat but chaff.

Stretching

Take a bolt of rich fabric,
the finest you could buy,
unwrap and unfasten it,
let it flow like a silken river
across your shop's floor
with a magical shine to it,
never seen even in dreams.

You pin one end down flat
so you can stretch the cloth,
take it farther than it was,
force the fabric longer still,
until the fine weave strains,
each thread begins to gasp,
then finally --- the cloth rips.

When material tears like this,
I tell you, it cannot be mended,
The pattern of warp and woof
is wrenched and so destroyed,
the threads hang like cut hair;
the cloth's body is dismembered,
only fit for limbs and ligaments.

So it was with my son's Order,
outgrowing its small shape,
stretched, wrenched, expanded,
torn into fractions and factions,
some defying their own founder.
The reports came to Francesco
who knew troubles waited ahead.

Earthquake

Years ago, Assisi's earth shook;
the road ahead seemed to ripple,
did the ground tilt for a moment?
So it appeared; my horse reared.

I reached my own shop in safety
but what it held left me stunned.
Bolts of cloth lay all over the floor;
most fabrics fell in new patterns.

For a moment, I felt overwhelmed.
No, it was days, it was many weeks.
A sea of spilled silks made me gasp.
Nothing, I knew, would be the same.

Years later, after his time in Egypt,
Francesco must have felt a shock:
His Order looking like my shop,
I would guess, after that tremor.

At first my son was not recognized;
new friars shut the doors in his face.
Finally, welcomed by his old friends,
my son faced a quake's aftermath.

His early vision was challenged.
Life at the Gospel's radical edge
did not fit the larger Order now --
more than five thousand strong.

Francesco refused to compromise.
He wrote a new Rule for the Order,
now organized into new provinces,
and announced one final decision.

For Shame

Sometimes I rue seeing the past.
Scenes flash up that make me mad.
I watch what I cannot now change.

An advantage to my situation is this:
A spirit can shout and no one hears.
I could say unspeakable things; I do.

I see my son lying ill, shaken by chills,
salt-white, clinging to his straw pallet.
Alone, I shout. *For shame, for shame.*

Three young friars, fairly new, talk on.
ignoring the pressing needs of my son.
They are annoyed by him, I can tell.

That angelic friar, Giles, appears now.
Iron gray hair, beard, keen blue eyes,
Francesco's defender from the start.

"I dreamed I visited Hell," a friar says.
"And I didn't see a single Franciscan."
"Go deeper next time," snaps Giles.

As I said, I don't think I am privileged
to see what lies behind the scenes.
I wish I could reach out to my child.

Shock

"From now on, I am dead to you:"
my son's hard words to his friars.
He resigned as the Order's head
and never regained that position.

The new generation of brothers,
with many of the older members,
helped reorganize the fraternity;
my son's design was reshaped.

Change is a constant, we know,
but Francesco's altered dream
must have felt like a surgery,
even if changes were needed.

"Lord, I give back to You this family
which until now you entrusted to me.
I can no longer take care of them...."
He remained the most humble of all.

Francesco knew his failings well.
His gift: Inspiration, not organization.
True it was; I speak from experience.
He sensed this and bent to the truth.

My son entered his last stage of life,
an entrance and an exit, with grace.
Now he was free for contemplation
in the mountain caves he so loved.

But he was sometimes forgotten,
often afraid of burdening others.
Francesco gave himself to prayer,
patient as he had not been earlier.

Francesco on Monte Verna

Did the earth rise to clasp his knees
as Francesco knelt in that *carcero,*
a cool mountain retreat above town;
gold-green hills sunning themselves,
hiding pockets of night deep within?

Didn't the cave walls lean toward him,
this homegrown son of ancient Assisi,
sheltering him as they arched above,
offering comfort, retreat, and release
from guilt, from shame, from failure.

I imagine him there as I stood outside,
listening to his passionate prayers,
self-accusations and newer resolves,
raised to the only One he called Father,
as I, like a spurned suitor, silently wept.

But if I had gone to my son in his pain,
I would not have known what to say.
We seemed above apologies by then;
our fractured bonds had yet to mend,
I thought, as I waited outside in the sun.

Who could put together, piece by piece,
this complex, God-struck, devoted man,
the child I never understood at all, I know,
and too late it was to begin healing now.
In those hills, together, apart, we mourned.

Trust

Suffering takes us beyond our landscape
without a map, a pathway or a guide.
We think it punishment for our mistakes
but we hold such hidden thoughts inside.

Holy men among us see it otherwise.
Francesco, in his final seven years,
knew rejection, illnesses and blindness,
but offered up his suffering, not tears.

Every living thing shares this condition,
hallowed by God's suffering with us.
We, a company of souls on mission,
soon or late may fight this or may trust.

If I am writing here what seems a lie,
choose trust for a day before you die.

On Faith

Maybe it falls over you
like sun through a veil;
like a dusting of pollen.

Or does it flatten you
like lightning's arrows,
a storm's slam of hail?

For some so it comes;
this I have heard, but
no bush burned for me.

Faith seeded my soul,
fed by pain, joy, prayer,
growing like a cypress.

The tree's green heft
reaching through me,
rising past my knees,

branching now, taller,
flexing and leafing,
roots stronger still.

I do not understand
what is happening
but it welcomes me.

Holy Wounds

Again, I watch Francesco kneel
in a cavern on his Monte Verna.
I see the white-hot intensity of
his love for God, always known,
in the dimming canopy of dusk,
in spreading yoke-yellow dawns,
but most keenly in the wounded
figure of the Crucified One, alone.

My son feels the wounds himself
as he prays in La Verna's peace,
where he asks to be united with
the suffering God-Man, rejected,
abandoned by his own disciples,
hanging like no more than meat,
taking on the weight of the world.

A fierce light, piercing blindness,
suddenly fills a slice of the sky --
then the vision, an angel aloft,
its luminous wings spread wide,
pinned bloodless onto the Cross.
Just then, Francesco has pain
in his hands, feet, and his side.
He is graced with Divine Union,
nailed on God's love, crucified.

From where I am now, I see
the look on my son's thin face
held a new and radiant ecstacy,
like a candle's furled inner heat.

This, the final blessing for him,
fills him with a wordless joy.
It is the sum of life for my boy.

Miracles

The dark descends
with a long black sigh
to cool the feverish air;
moistening dry ground
with its maligned mercy.

In night's darkest core,
in its secret marrow,
hidden from daylight's
long probing fingers,
its unblinking eyes,

miracles may open as
night-blooming flowers,
unseen or understood.
But they scent the air
even before we notice.

They blossom while
we pass their borders
and smell their perfume.
Tonight we can't guess
when a miracle opens,

like secret blossoms
giving their own scent
to the air at our windows,
as we close the shutters
and put out the lights.

Duet

At night, in my dreams,
I converse with my son.
Every time, it's the same.
I start. "Why did you go?"
　"I had a new life," he says.
"Why not as a monk?" I ask.
　"That wasn't my calling."
"Restoring the Church?"
　"Yes, and more," he says.
"Then what, Francesco?"
　"To live like a disciple."
"And like your Master," I add.
　We are silent a while.
"I see better now," I tell him.
　"And so do I," he says.
"I wronged you," I admit.
　"I renounced you," he says.
"Why did we part for so long?"
　"I feared you," he said.
"I was so angry," I confess.
　"I had my faults," he sighs.
We sit in the quiet again.
"I watched you," I say then.
　"I know," Francesco nods.
"You watched me, too?"
　"How could I ever stop?"
"I was proud of you, son."
　"Were you?" He's amazed.
I nod. "You gave me that."
　"I gave you grief," he says.
"You remember the lake?"
　"Every day. We have that."
"We do." My voice cracks.
He is too weak to speak
I am too joyous to weep.

In the Dark

How could a child of mine go blind?
I shouted at God in grief and rage.
No quarrel can erase a parent's pain
for one he seeded, watered, raised.
I thought I hated my Francesco ---
so blotting out my hatred for myself.
Why did I still ache for him, for us,
even here where I waft in eternity?

A bitter thing it is to be helpless,
as all parents are, to avert harm,
cool the fever, mend the wounds,
disarm the danger, foil the plot.
When life disrupts our children,
we all feel that attack ourselves,
and feel it inwardly, piercing us
in each heartbeat, every bone.

My son had slowly lost his sight.
His eyes gave him knife-like pain;
patient, brave, he clung to prayer.
In agony, he managed to compose
his hymn, *Canticle of the Creatures,*
offering his highest praise to God.
After that, he was lost in a twilight,
dawn and day and noon and night.
At forty-three, he'd aged too soon.

In Francesco's growing darkness,
what else did the blind man see
beside the waning sunflowers,
dimming cypress, fading grass?
I suppose he saw as the blind do,
inner worlds and worlds beyond.
Maybe he sees miracles we miss.

Silk

Now I want to wade into the waters
of forgetfulness, where I can escape
my wild mind's continued disorder
to deeper, bluer, newer simpler days.

Back then, life was a bolt of flawless silk,
an easy one to purchase or to sell.
Francesco, a child, only cried for milk,
I thought, blind to the spirit in his shell.

Now he is blind and I, the spirit, weep,
wishing myself back to that brief time,
recreating all of it --- but differently.
Instead, the present is a hill to climb.

Hindsight is a wise but brutal teacher.
It asks all the courage of the creature.

In Sight

Now that my son is blind,
the blind man who sees
what few of us ever will,
his eyes are red as sunset,
his legs, once muscled oak,
taking him on miles of road,
had weakened, willow-thin.
He'd cut stone, built churches
the staunch gates of Assisi
for God, he would have said:
Create to praise the Creator.

Mason, musician, mystic --
my son remained a mystery
and I, a mystery to myself.
Something softened in me
when Francesco went blind.
As he lost all of his sight,
I gained some of my own.
I saw my son led by Giles.
And I wished it was by me.

A cruel thing it is for any parent
to see his child gasp in suffering.
As Francesco rested on his litter
he stirred, smiling for a moment.
I wonder if he knew I was there,
a spirit in that grove of silence,
father and son together again,
mutely forgiving, no words now.
For me, for him, it was enough.

Epiphany

Only now that I am dead I come alive
to feel the arrowhead of love within,
never felt when I was enclosed by skin.
With my departure I at last arrived.
Why did it take me decades to attain
this state of devotion, pleated with pain?

I hover here to watch my son, asleep,
between ongoing twists of agony.
I want to take all of them upon me.
Throughout my life, I refused to weep.
Love without sacrifice is what we seek
but one without the other is too weak.

Strong, not tender: so I saw myself.
God's love was my son's main belief,
but I could not share it, to my grief.
In truth, belief was never my wealth.
No sermon could dent my own pride.
I kept disbelief under my tough hide.

You see what it took to alter my sight.
A vigil with my ailing child changed all.
It is a brutal way to learn, as I recall.
How hard we work to escape the light.
I saw God, the loving Father, as I cared
more for my son than I had ever dared,

Last Days

Look at the man I call my son:
Blind, weak, feverish, pained,
stomach ulcers, sores on skin.
Even now it hurts to watch him.

His eyelids like attentive moths,
fluttering when left unbandaged.
Does he think of his childhood
between sighs, deeper prayer?

That day we waded into a lake,
he, excited, maybe three, four,
staggering, splashing, tottering,
holding me, both of us laughing.

Or is that what I, the father, see?
Are we both watching one picture?
Me, swinging him, both crowing,
skimming the lake's blue blanket.

Francesco, I know, sees the Cross;
he leans on the love of God alone
Who holds him, skimming the top
of all the lake-water in the world.

My son, stirring now, awake again,
needing care almost all the time:
A burden to some of his brothers,
Francesco hears what they say.

He is slipping farther away, I see,
as if in the lake where I held him,
his heart beating fast against me.
Now the beats are slowing, slowing.

Night Timing

Sky's fire dies.
Sun, a closing eye;
trees burn out
leaving ash.

Night a wing,
pinned in place
by small tacks
of a billion lights.

Feeling time run
in its hour-glass
sifting the sands
for my son and I.

Morning listens
for its first note.
The sleepless
craving light.

Shutters open,
earth awakens.
Sun an open eye.
Will he die today?

Night's thin layer
losing its place,
falling faster now.
Its time expires as

each
pin
drops
out.

Waning

It is my son's time to die.
He knows it, we know it.
The look of death on him,
the waning of this thin man,
like the last sliver of moon,
is a quiet thing, accepted,
in union with all that live,
and with the suffering God.

Uneasy, though, his mind
about leaving all his friars
yet unsettled, as they are.
Francesco did as God asked;
he knows well his friends
will do as God asks them.
He must let go and he does.

Why do I think of dawn
in the twilight of this life?
How the sky turns milky,
then the first new blue
of a waking infant's eyes.
Is this death or is it birth
I am given to attend here?
God and Francesco know.

He murmurs one psalm:
"I call upon You, O Lord..."
His voice a whisper now:
"... come quickly to me..."
The whisper reedy, thin:
"In You I seek refuge...."
Still Francesco prays:
"...do not leave me...."

Gathering Larks

I peer through time's windows to watch
my dying son laid naked on the ground,
at his request, by his four closet friends,
keeping vigil with Francesco to the last.

There he lies like a newborn in man's skin.
He turns to the earth as he came into it,
marking this time as his rebirth to new life,
awaited as he leans on nothing but his God.

I see him as a naked baby, squalling in my arms.
As a child, bathing. That day at Lake Trasimeno.
These images flash up fast, one after the other.
And one more, the sight I have tried to forget:

I see the young man I had raised stripping naked,
giving over clothes and coins and renouncing me.
At the start of his ministry, Francesco was bare,
as he is now, at the end of his calling and his life.

Looking down on him, almost a skeleton already,
I sense a faint warmth seep throughout my spirit,
almost like the feel of blood I used to know in life.
Again, I'm forgiving him, again he's forgiving me.

Dusk falling. Francesco dry lips are moving still.
Sudden birdsong: his beloved larks gathering now,
wheeling over the roof of the small hut, his own cell.
He must hear. Friends hold his hands. He is gone.

Vigil

Candles wavering
through the night:
another vigil kept.
Morning, too soon.

The body of my son
carried on a rope litter
to Lady Clare's convent.
She offers her farewell.

Moving on then, in step,
all the brothers walking
in pairs, follow the litter
a long way to the grave.

No one can see me but
I am in this procession.
I have followed that litter
with the whole of my soul

And so I am, in the end,
or at this new beginning,
a true follower of my son,
      Francis of Assisi.

For Francesco from Pietro

My fingers, tracing threads of your life,
discovered a soul richer than its weave,
its greatness lost to me, at first, in strife;
or this omission I continually grieve.

You are the father now and I the son,
learning still what it means to be a saint;
mine the rougher fabric, yours finespun,
all offered up to God without restraint.

In the shadows of obscurity you died
where you had lived, oblivious to fame
and unaware, that autumn eventide,
how the world waited to sing your name.

You showed us a glimmer of the Mystery
glancing off our small lives for centuries.

Pietro Admits

Let me say I enjoyed my resentments
until my son showed me how much they cost.
Righteousness brought me deep contentment
until being right caused my greatest loss.

His dream of knighthood was mine, I believe,
I foisted my own ambitions on him.
He had to escape them so he had to leave.
He was repentant for years as for sin.

I study his patterns more closely now
that the circle has made it full turning.
Dependence on God: that was his vow.
I wonder if I have yet started learning.

Thanks to my son for all he has been.
At last I am proud to have fathered him.

At Dusk

Candle-lighting time.
Lamp-lighting time.

Magical even now
as our windows

cut button-holes
in the darkness.

How many candles
have I lit in my life?

In church, at times.
At the table, always.

Now our poor lights
will mirror the stars,

held in their courses
by the Lord's hand,

remaining so bright
by the great Mystery.

Birds know all this.
Why is it we forget?

Do this as I pass on:
Light a candle for me.

EPILOGUE

Departure

Now my time to remain here is finished.
This penance gave me pain and peace.
Cheap it is if it comes readily, with ease.
Humbled, yes, but I am not diminished.
In death alone I knew my own son's life.
May this end for him, for me, all strife.

Eternity may shock you with its size --
a hangar for us and our ugly loose ends.
These seem to be anything but friends,
yet clipping them would not be advised.
It takes nerve to handle such threads;
worse to stock your afterlife with dread.

If you, too, move ahead by looking back,
it is peace with the past you may find,
settling rages and regrets in your mind.
From love no fault nor flaw may detract.
Hindsight waits to lead you out of night.
To avoid my fate, reach out for the light.

+++

APPENDIX

Author's Note

This book is fiction, not biography or hagiography.
It is a series of linked poems that tell a story and was
designed to be read in sequence, if possible.

Its artistic form is related to the long tradition of poetry
integrated with story or visa versa. Humbly, very
humbly, I cite Medieval "verse stories," troubadours'
song, the Gliards (itinerant poet-musicians) throughout
Europe and Britain.

An important note on names: Saint Francis was
baptized "Giovanni" but was always known as
"Francesco," his father's wish. **The *original* name for
"Francis" *is* "Francesco"** which is also the Italian
version. I have used the latter; it is the name the
narrator would have chosen. "Francis" is an
English/Latin form of "Francesco."

The saint is often a "birdbath sculpture" and was indeed
a great lover of Nature. It is also important to emphasize
his roles as the founder of a social movement, an
important religious Order and as a devout man of faith.
Francis undertook a radical approach to living the
Gospels, as counter-cultural today as it was in the
Middle Ages.

This book is based on historical facts regarding many
events in the life of Francis and his father, Pietro
Bernardone, who is traditionally cast as a villain. No
reliable birth nor death dates exist for him. He is this
story's "*narrator*," a point-of-view which *differentiates*
this work from others.

Pietro traveled widely on business. He learned cultured
speech from his noble clients, if not from his boyhood.

His wife, Pica, was said to be a noble from Provence, France. Sources refer to Pietro's love of poetic songs, a love he shared with his son. The mutual renunciation of parent and son is usually reported as a public event.

There are many conflicting sources and chronologies for Saint Francis. As an author of historical fiction (Saint Joan, Mother Seton) I have had to make choices.

The stories of the Gubbio wolf and the sermon to the birds are considered legend by some biographers. However, these stories are integral parts of the Franciscan tradition, so I have included them.

Francis is often credited with originating the first Christmas crib or crèche. Actually, this custom was already observed in Rome, but Francis made a *tableau vivant* in Greccio, Italy.

References to the sermon with ashes, the rosebush (or brambles), the broom, the moon, the fast/feast, the gamblers and the lepers are also sourced, although the leper's embrace is often described as a kiss. The meetings with the Sultan, alMalek al-Kamil and Cardinal Pelgius are referenced in all sources, as are activities in Egypt. Lady Chiara, the future Saint Clare, did meet on occasion with Francis but never alone. As Abbess, her convent was located at San Damiano.

A note on quotes: Those from Saint Francis are attributed; some are slightly paraphrased. A handful of poems appear here in different forms from my books, *Where Do Things Go* and *A Misplaced Woman.* I used the term "Franciscans" for reader recognition but they were originally "The Friars Minor."

A note on language: Stage terms go back to the widespread presence of pageant-plays and secular plays. Some words, such as "crook," sound modern but were in Medieval usage. Buttons were used in the twelfth century. In any case, they are cited by a character "beyond" time as we know it.

I gratefully acknowledge the many sources I have used, especially the excellent works of Rev. Murray Bodo OFM, Thomas de Celano, and Donald Spoto. (See Bibliography).

Marcy Heidish, July 2020

The Historical Context

Assisi is in Umbria, an inland region in the mid-section of Italy. The town, built on a slope of Mount Subasio, was founded by the Umbrians about 1000 BC and further developed by the Romans circa 250 BC. When Saint Francis was born about 1182, Assisi's middle and merchant classes were thriving.

Italy was then comprised of independent city-states, frequently battling one another. This was the era of the Crusades, glorified warfare, courtly poetry, chivalry and cathedral-building. The Church was powerful and rich. Many of its clerics were characterized as immoral, corrupt and materialistic. Noble families feuded. The rising middle and merchant classes prospered. Money was newly valued as a possession, not only as a means of commerce.

One flourishing merchant was Pietro di Bernardone, importer and purveyor of expensive fabrics and, arguably, the wealthiest man in Assisi. Probably in 1182, his French wife, Pica, gave birth to a son, baptized "Giovanni." However, the child was always called Francesco or Francis, interchangeably, at his father's wish. Very much in the background was Angelo, a half-brother from Pica's previous marriage in France.

All sources agree that both parents indulged and spoiled Francis/Francesco. Early on, he enjoyed a privileged lifestyle, expensive clothing, and a youth spent in late-night revelry with his friends, who benefitted from his generosity.

In 1202, during a battle between Assisi and Perugia, Francis was captured by the Perugians and held as a prisoner of war in a dank jail. A year later, Pietro was able to ransom his son. Francis was ill for another year (probably with malaria). Once recovered, he set out to be a knight, but twenty miles from home, he experienced a strong mystical compunction to turn back. After his return to Assisi, Francis lost his taste for revelry. In town, he was sometimes called a coward or a madman.

He wandered the woods and hills, meditating on what to do with his life. During this period, he came upon a leper or lepers. Repulsive, ill, odiferous, regarded as cursed, they were avoided by all, including Francis in his early days. This time, however, he felt moved to embrace and care for these outcasts. He saw in them the wounded, dying, abandoned Christ; perhaps he also saw himself. His ministry to lepers was lifelong.

Again, in his wanderings, Francis found San Damiano, a small, abandoned, half-ruined church, just outside Assisi's walls. Praying before its large and beautiful Crucifix, he felt or heard a personal call to "...*repair My house [or "Church] as it is falling into ruin.*" Francis himself sensed a "*mysterious inner change,*" but did not realize the larger scope of his commission then.

By the end of 1205, Francis left home to live at San Damiano. To raise funds for its restoration, Francis took a large portion of his father's inventory and sold it in another town. He brought the profits to San Damiano but its priest refused the money.

Enraged and concerned for his son's sanity, the business, and money set aside for Francis's inheritance, Pietro chained his son and locked him in a storeroom. Pica released Francis who left again. When her husband came back from a journey, Pietro demanded restitution for theft.

According to most sources, the adjudication of this problem was public (1206), decided by Assisi's Bishop Guido. Francis, after returning the money, stripped to return all clothing from his father, denied his paternity and was disinherited. After one more reference, Pietro and Pica disappear from history.

Francis continued to live simply at San Damiano. He labored to restore it, cared for lepers and spent much time in prayer. He went to Mass every morning, did menial day jobs and, when needed, sought alms for building stones. For two years he lived as a kind of penitential hermit. At that time he had no intention of founding a religious order.

In 1208, two voluntary followers came to Francis. In 1209, there were a few more. The men moved into a vacant shed on a river (Rivo Torto) where they lived as Francis did. Their "Rule" or "Form of Life" was based on texts from the Gospels. In 1209, they went to Rome where they sought and received verbal approval for their "Rule" from Pope Innocent III.

Around 1211, a Benedictine Monastery gave Francis and his "Friars Minor" a tiny chapel, the Porziuncola, with some surrounding land. (An alternate spelling is "Porziuncula"). Several more men joined the friars. Handmade mud-and-wattle huts, adjoining the chapel, housed them. They marked the backs of their plain tunics with a *tau* formed by a **T**, the last letter in the Greek and Hebrew alphabets, in a shape evocative of the Cross. This became the Franciscans' emblem.

In 1212 Chiara (Clare) di Favarone, inspired by the preaching of Francis, ran away from her wealthy and aristocratic family to give her life to God. Francis helped her to begin her journey. She became abbess of a Franciscan Order for women, now "The Poor Clares."

They lived in enclosure at San Damiano.

The movement begun by Francis grew so popular, a Third Order was created for lay people, or Secular Franciscans.

Starting in 1209, Francis and his "band of brothers" preached in the streets and piazzas of towns throughout Europe. The friars went out to the people, where they lived and worked, spoke in the vernacular, dressed plainly, and emphasized not only repentance but God's mercy and love.

And they had Francis. All sources note his joyous demeanor, his charisma, his gentleness and, above all, his religious devotion. Some sources regard as legend the stories of Francis's sermon to the birds and his taming of a wolf, but I have included them as part of the Franciscan tradition.

There are other idiosyncratic stories that are well-sourced, including those about the moon, the broom, the gamblers, the ashes, the midnight supper and Francs's dying wish to lie naked on the earth.

It must be said that Francis was counter-cultural. He took a radical approach to living the Gospels. Francis espoused a "God-centered" life of simplicity, poverty, humility, peacemaking, and service to the poor and sick. He believed these values honored God and gave life true meaning. Also, it was available to everyone, not only monastics or clergy.

These values contrasted sharply with the medieval glorification of war, wealth, status, rich clothing and possessions, an elite clergy and a lifestyle, devoid of service. And yet the

Franciscan movement grew rapidly. About 5,000 friars gathered in 1217 to discuss ways of organizing their increasing numbers.

In 1219, Francis sailed to Egypt and met with its Sultan, Malek al-Kamil. Both leaders wanted a peaceful end to the horrific slaughter of the Fifth Crusade. The Sultan, a cultured and thoughtful ruler, recognized the Italian friar as a holy man. Francis, unarmed, went behind the battle lines to preach peace. Although the crusaders' commander rejected a truce, the respectful interfaith dialogue between Francis and Malek alKamil was groundbreaking and remains topical today.

When Francis returned to Assisi, he was dangerously ill and his Order was in turmoil. Francis refused the demands for a more traditional monastic life. His radical approach to living the Gospel was rejected by the majority. Francis saw his original values diluted as his Order took a different shape.

In 1221 he wrote a new Rule. (A revision, called the "Later Rule," written in 1223, was approved by Pope Honorius III). However, many of the younger, newer friars neither honored Francis nor his vision. He no longer held the respect he had in earlier years. The community was in danger of a split.

To avert such a split, Francis resigned as General of the Order. His position was less secure. His last four years were dominated by an agonizing eye disease (probably trachoma) and virtual blindness. He suffered from other serious ailments; all attempted cures failed. Some friars resented the care Francis required. Increasingly isolated and ill, he was patient in suffering and in prayer.

In 1224, during a vision, Francis became the Church's first Stigmatic. He experienced in his body the wounds of the Crucified Christ, to whom he was always devoted. He had tried to live as Jesus did and this mystical experience was the culmination of that desire. There has been some debate about the nature of the wounds, but I have taken the traditional view.

Despite disappointments, rejection, disease and debilitation, Francis wrote (or dictated) a famous hymn of praise to God, "*Canticle of the Creatures*" (1225). We must note that the well known "Peace Prayer" first appeared anonymously in a small periodical in 1912, but it reflects the spirit and values of Francis of Assisi.

Surrounded by his closest friends, he slipped toward death. For a brief time these friends did fulfill his dying request, to lie stripped on the earth. He also broke and blessed bread, distributing it to his friends as Jesus did at the Last Supper.

At dusk, on October 3rd, 1226, Francis died in his cell adjoining the Porziuncola. As he died he whispered Psalm 141; his two closet friends held his hands. An "exaltation" of larks, his favorite bird, wheeled in low circles over his roof as they sang. Eyewitnesses report this event. Francis was about forty-four years old.

His funeral procession passed Lady Clare's window so she could make a silent farewell. Francis was buried in Assisi and canonized a saint by the Catholic Church in 1228. His remains were later re-interred in a newly built Basilica dedicated to him, a popular destination for pilgrims to this day. Saint Francis continues to be one of the most beloved holy personages in the world.

Marcy Heidish, 2020
www.marcyheidishbooks.com

Canticle of the Creatures
By Saint Francis of Assisi, 1225

Most High, all powerful, good Lord,
Yours are the praises, the glory, the honor,
and all blessing.

To You alone, Most High, do they belong,
and no man is worthy to mention Your name.

Be praised, my Lord, through all your creatures,
especially through my lord Brother Sun,
who brings the day; and you give light through him.
And he is beautiful and radiant in all his splendor!
Of you, Most High, he bears the likeness.

Praised be You, my Lord, through Sister Moon
and the stars, in heaven you formed them
clear and precious and beautiful.

Praised be You, my Lord, through Brother Wind,
and through the air, cloudy and serene,
and every kind of weather through which
You give sustenance to Your creatures.

Praised be You, my Lord, through Sister Water,
which is very useful and humble and precious and
chaste.

Praised be You, my Lord, through Brother Fire,
through whom you light the night and he is beautiful
and playful and robust and strong.

Praised be You, my Lord, through Sister Mother Earth,
who sustains us and governs us and who produces
varied fruits with colored flowers and herbs.

Praised be You, my Lord,
through those who give pardon for Your love,
and bear infirmity and tribulation.

Blessed are those who endure in peace
for by You, Most High, they shall be crowned.

Praised be You, my Lord,
through our Sister Bodily Death,
from whom no living man can escape.

Woe to those who die in mortal sin.
Blessed are those whom death will
find in Your most holy will,
for the second death shall do them no harm.

Praise and bless my Lord,
and give Him thanks
and serve Him with great humility.

(Translation by the Franciscan Friars Third Order
Regular)

Prayer Attributed to Saint Francis *

Lord, make me an instrument of your peace.
Where there is hatred, let me bring love.
Where there is offense, let me bring pardon.
Where there is discord, let me bring union.
Where there is error, let me bring truth.
Where there is doubt, let me bring faith.
Where there is despair, let me bring hope.
Where there is darkness, let me bring your light.
Where there is sadness, let me bring joy.
O Master, let me not seek as much
to be consoled as to console,
to be understood as to understand,
to be loved as to love,
for it is in giving that one receives,
it is in self-forgetting that one finds,
it is in pardoning that one is pardoned,
it is in dying that one is raised to eternal life.

● **Original 1912 version, translated from the French, copyright expired.**

Select Abbreviated Bibliography

PRINT:

Bonaventure, Saint, *The Life of St. Francis of Assisi* (Tan Classics) Apr 1, 2010, Publisher: Saint Benedict Press, LLC.

Bodo, Murray, O.F.M., *Francis: The Journey and the Dream*, Chicago: St. Anthony Messenger Press, c1988.

----- *The Way of St. Francis*, Garden City, NY: Doubleday, 1984.

Boff, Leonardo, *The Prayer of Saint Francis*, New York: Orbis, 2001.

Chesterton, G. K. (Gilbert Keith), 1874-1936., *Saint Francis of Assisi / G.K. Chesterton*, Brewster, Mass., Paraclete Press, 2009.

----- *St. Thomas Aquinas / G.K. Chesterton*; with an introduction by **Ralph McInerny**, St. Francis of Assisi / with an introduction by **Joseph Pearce**, San Francisco, CA.: Ignatius Press, 2002.

Englebert, Omer: *St. Francis of Assisi: a biography*, Second English Edition, revised and augmented by Ignatius Brady, O.F.M., and Raphael Brown, Cincinnati, Ohio: Servant Books, an imprint of Franciscan Media, 2013. Originally published: Chicago: Franciscan Herald Press, 1966. Translation by Eve Marie Cooper

Francke, Linda Bird, *On the Road with Francis of Assisi*, New York: Random House, 2005.

Short, William, *The Franciscans*, Wilmington, Del.; Michael Glazier, 1989.

Smith, Huston, *Why Religion Matters: The Fate of the Human Spirit in an Age of Disbelief*, San Francisco: HarperSanFrancisco, 2001.

Smith, John Holland, *Francis of Assisi*, New York, Charles Scribner's Sons, 1972.

Spoto, Donald, 1941- , *Reluctant Saint: the Life of Francis of Assisi*, New York: Viking Compass, 2002.

Sweeney, Jon M.: *Francis of Assisi in His Own Words: The Essential Writings*, Apr 28, 2013; translated, introduced, and annotated by Jon M. Sweeney, Brewster, Mass.: Paraclete Press.

----- *The Complete Francis of Assisi: His Life, The Complete Writings and The Little Flowers* (Paraclete Giants), Aug 1, 2015

Thomas, of Celano, *Life of our blessed Father Francis / Thomas of Celano*; translated by Timothy Johnson, PhD., St. Bonaventure: Franciscan Institute Publications, 2016; (Contemporary of St. Francis, 1st biography after Francis's death.)

----- *St. Francis of Assisi*: first and second life of St. Francis with selections from the Treatise on the miracles of blessed Francis; translated from the Latin with introduction and footnotes by Placid Hermann; Chicago, Ill.: Franciscan Herald Press, c1988.

----- *The Francis Trilogy of Thomas of Celano*, Edited by Regis J. Armstrong, OFM Cap., J. A. Wayne Hellman, OFM Conv., William J. Short, OFM, foreword by Regis J. Armstrong, OFM Cap., NY: New City Press, 2004.

Thompson, Augustine, O.P., *Francis of Assisi, A New Biography*, Cornell University, 2012.

Trxler, Richard C., *Naked Before the Father; The Renunciation of Francis of Assisi*, vol. 9, New York: Peter Lang, 1989.

Warren, Kathleen, *Daring to Cross the Threshold: Francis of Assisi Encounters Malek Al-Kamil*, Aug 21, 2012.

DVD/FILM:
Assisi: Home of St. Francis, 2004, Janson Media DVD, Release Date: July 12, 2016.

Clare and Francis, Ignatius Press, 2008.

The Sultan and the Saint, The Story of the Sultan of Egypt and Francis of Assisi, 2017 Unity Productions, PBS Distribution.

A WOMAN CALLED MOSES
*Houghton Mifflin Co., Original Publisher

*Award-winning, best-selling novel based on the life of Harriet Tubman, abolitionist and conductor on the Underground Railroad.

*Literary Guild Alternate Selection; *A Bantam paperback.

*TV Movie, starring Cicely Tyson, still available on DVD.

Praise for *A Woman Called Moses*:
Publishers Weekly: "Her story has been told before, but never as eloquently, almost poetically, as here...achingly real...a strong narrative of a totally committed woman, one who speaks directly to our own desperate need to feel committed—and our wish that somewhere in the world there were more people like Harriet Tubman."

Washington Post Book World: "Profoundly rewarding...a daring work of the imagination."

Chicago Sun Times: "Marcy Heidish has, almost uncannily, crawled into the skin and very mind of Harriet Tubman. The dialogue sings with poetic beauty."

Houghton Mifflin Co.: "As events build toward a stunning climax, we are drawn into the spellbinding narrative of an extraordinary life, and a portion of our American past."

WITNESSES
Houghton Mifflin Co., Original Publisher

A Novel By Marcy Heidish

Award-winning novel based on the life of lay minister Anne Hutchinson, <u>America's first female advocate of religious freedom</u>.

Citations: Society for Colonial Wars; laudatory reviews;

large-print, hard-cover and paperback versions.

Praise for *Witnesses:*

The New York Times Book Review: "...nothing ordinary about her creation of this remarkable woman. The novel abounds in literary grace. It employs the voices of the times as though heard this minute."

The New Yorker Magazine: "A striking novel...a compelling portrait."

The Washington Post: "Pure pleasure. Anne Hutchinson is real; thanks to *Witnesses,* she at last assumes her proper place in American history." —Jonathan Yardley, Pulitzer Prizewinning critic.

Ballantine Books: "This fearless woman, mother of fifteen, a leader in medicine and politics, comes to vivid life in these pages. A true believe in religious freedom who paid dearly for her principles in two trials for heresy. In the tradition of Arthur Miller's *The Crucible*, Witnesses is the deeply felt portrait of a woman in the paranoid climate of 17th century Boston."

THE TORCHING—The Book Store Murders
Simon & Schuster, Original Publisher

- Acclaimed contemporary novel, in hardcover and paperback

- Literary Guild Alternate

  Optioned for TV movie.

Praise for *The Torching*:

Washington Post Book World:
"Because of Heidish's skill, we get the full force of her double-whammy, in part due to the grace with which she weaves the present day and the historical, but also because of her inventiveness at the book's close, the daring way she gets both strands of plot to unite... a stylish and intelligent novelist to boot, more than up to the dizzying, tale-spinning task that she set for herself here."

Kirkus Reviews: "Shuddery mystery- suspense with supernatural overtones."

Library Journal: "Intricately constructed. A deliciously spine-tingling, multi-layered literary mystery."

Publishers Weekly: "Subtle, gratifying psychological suspense. Penetrating characterizations...Heidish impeccably orchestrates the historical and contemporary, the supernatural and psychological."

Denver Post: "Macabre ride...Eerie. Intriguing. Frightening surprises...Enjoy."

Arizona Daily Star: "An imaginative, amazing writer...A magician with words."

New York Daily News: "Compellingly readable and likely to induce the screaming-meemies."

THE SECRET ANNIE OAKLEY
New American Library, Original Publisher

Acclaimed novel based on the life of the legendary sharp-shooter.

Hard- & Paperback versions

A *Readers Digest* Condensed Novel.

Optioned for film.

*Translated into several languages, laudatory reviews.

Praise for *The Secret Annie Oakley:*

Kirkus Reviews: "An immensely touching and cohesive fictional biography of the legendary sharp-shooter, builds from exemplary research to a fresh portrait of a talented woman in crisis, a class act—as Heidish reconstructs. with color and drama, the choreography of the shows, the tone of the period, and the textures of a haunting past."

The Arizona Daily Star: "...an imaginative, amazing writer, a magician with words. Each character has been brought to life with a mere pen stroke; flesh and blood beings that are more than fiction. A master-piece of creatlve wrltlng."

The Kansas City Star: "An unforgettable story."

Christian Science Monitor: "...Marcy Heidish weaves historical facts into a novel so moving that there will be many times in the years to come that I'll take pleasure in remembering that stout-hearted woman. Annie Oakley' hits the bull's eye every time."

MIRACLES

New American Library, Original Publisher

Historical novel based on the life of **Mother Elizabeth Set on**, first American born canonized saint.

Main selection, *The Catholic Book Club.*

Praise for *Miracles*:

The New York Times Book Review: "This appealing book, told from the point of view of a skeptical modern priest, moves swiftly through tragedy to triumph."

Kirkus Reviews: "Working delicately with a balance of Church hagiography and psychological insight, Ms. Heidish provides another strong focus on the root dilemma of female saints and achievers."

New American Library: "*Miracles* is the story of an unforgettable woman's life and love. It is a novel charged with the vitality of a life that saw many changes, and with the power of a love that took many forms.[whether] as a lonely daughter of a wealthy, indifferent man; a searching young woman; a contented matron embracing a marriage that produced five beloved children; a widow searching for new meaning to life."

DEADLINE
St. Martin's Press, Original Publisher

Contemporary psychological novel with a mystery" as a narrative line.

Nominee for prestigious Edgar" Award; fine reviews.

Praise for *Deadline*:

Washington Post: "*Deadline* is a tense, well-turned tale, filled with authentic police and newspaper people. Heidish's taut, punchy style moves the story at lightning speed."

Kirkus Reviews: "The high-tension plot is enhanced by sharply etched pictures, by many vivid characters, and by a crisp, clean, first-person style. Heidish imbues her haunting story and her gutsy heroine with a rare sense of tenderness and poignancy. An impressive mystery by a gifted writer."

St. Martin's Press: "This wire-tight novel probes relentlessly, driving deep into psychological darkness and violent death. As the riveting story reaches its stunning conclusion, we see a complex woman forced to meet the ultimate deadline."

A Dangerous Woman: Mother Jones, An Unsung American Heroine

*A compelling, inspiring new historical novel, another powerful "profile in courage" American-style novel based on the life of Mary Harris Jones, a self-proclaimed Hell Raiser, a daring labor leader, and colorful, quirky humanitarian.

*The arresting novel of an indomitable force, dressed demurely in widow's weeds and lace collars who:

> As an Irish immigrant—I lost her homeland to the Great Famine.

> As a wife and mother—lost her whole family to yellow fever.

> As a dressmaker—lost home and business to the Chicago Fire > As a survivor—turned from sorrow to help others survive.

Follow one of America's most feisty, fearless and forgotten heroines whose rallying cry was:

"PRAY FOR THE DEAD — AND FIGHT LIKE HELL FOR THE LIVING!"

DESTINED TO DANCE: A Novel About Martha Graham

> They called her a genius.

> They called her a goddess.

> They called her a monster.

Which title best fits Martha Graham, iconic Mother of Modern Dance?

Find out—in the first historical novel about this great American diva.

DESTINED TO DANCE is a creative portrait of the legendary dancer and choreographer. Heidish offers another remarkable account of an American heroine: her successes, her sorrows, and her struggles.

Here is a masterful portrait of Graham, on stage, backstage, offstage. We see Graham's break-through brilliance, often compared to Picasso's or Stravinsky.

We also witness Graham's triumph over alcoholism, despair, and a failed marriage. Set against the intriguing world of dance, Martha Graham's story offers us a close-up on a complex and compelling overcomer.

Martha Graham (1894-1991) invented a new "language of movement," still taught around the world and exemplified in such classic works as *Appalachian Spring*, among 180 others.

As always, Heidish's research is thorough and her sense of her subject is magical. For all who love the arts, all who seek inspiration, and all who like to read between history's lines, *DESTINED TO DANCE* is a must-read book.

Scene Through A Window
An Historical Romance

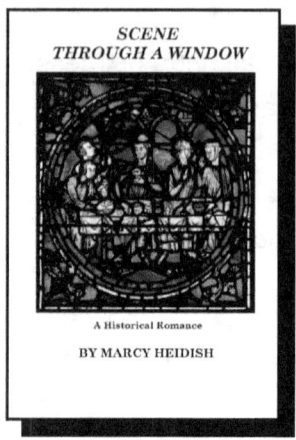

Travel through the centuries to watch a timeless love unfold around a timeless masterpiece: the fabled cathedral of Chartres, France. In 1194, an unthinkable disaster struck that sacred site. In one June night, a firestorm devastated the cathedral, its artwork, and parts of its surrounding town.

Immediately, the finest artists converged on Chartres to plan a new and innovative structure, built to endure and to surpass all that went before. Inevitably, these plans led to plots and rivalry, threatening the realization of a daring and demanding dream.

Against this backdrop, two lovers struggle to conceive the new cathedral's stained glass windows, still regarded as marvels today. This quest centers on discovering new gem-like colors: unique, precious, and incomparable. The pair, under increasing pressure, embarks on an intense search for the mysterious but elusive answers

Deftly weaving fact with fiction, Marcy Heidish sets an inspirational love story against a thoroughly researched Medieval backdrop. With her proven attention to detail, Heidish transports us to the winding streets of Chartres: its sounds and smells, its interiors and intrigues. Suspenseful, engrossing, and imaginative, **Scene Through A Window** creates a magical space where the impossible can happen.

Soul and the City

Waterproof Press (Random House imprint)

Praise for *Soul and the City*:

* I actually started reading Marcy Heidish's *Soul and the City* on a subway train. I must say it had exactly the effect she writes about: it gave me peace in the middle of the hurry, the rush, the loud noise of the city."
—Rick Hailin, executive editor, Guideposts; author of *Finding God on the A Train*

Marcy Heidish has compiled a rich and nuance touring companion to rival any Michelin or Eye-witness guide—usable in any city of the world. Keep it close and you will meet beauty and holiness no matter where you pause to look."
— Leigh McLeroy, author of *The Beautiful Ache* and *The Sacred Ordinary*

Soul and the City is a deeply inspiring call to awareness to connection with God and with others, and ultimately to soulful worship through so many aspects of life in the city that we find mundane, undesirable, or that even go unnoticed. Almost instantly, upon delving into its pages, you find your perspective changed."
— *Sarah Zacharias Davis, author of Confessions from an Honest Wife, Transparent, and The Friends We Keep.*

Defiant Daughters

Liguori Publications.

What do Joan of Arc, Immaculée Ilibagiza, Corrie ten Boom, and Sojourner Truth **have in common?**

These women are among those whom best-selling author Marcy Heidish calls "Defiant Daughters."

This informative, challenging, and entertaining book spotlights the lives of more than 20 spiritual trail-blazers and their responses to crises of conscience.

They represent different races, denominations, and nations, but all are feisty — often fiery — and always faithful to their callings.

Heidish seeks out the decisive juncture where each took a stand for conscience, however high the cost.

This stunning and compelling book will bring you face-to-face with an unforgettable female gallery of "profiles in courage."

— Liguori Publications

A Candle At Midnight

Ave Maria Press, Original Publisher

Praise for <u>A Candle At Midnight</u>:

Heidish honors modern medicine and spiritual healing in this compelling work."

— Alen J. Salerian, M.D., Medical Director of the Washing-ton Psychiatric Center

This is not a book of abstractions. I recommend this book to anyone who is caught in the darkness of mid-night."
— Martha Manning, Author of
Undercurrents: A Life Beneath the Surface:

A masterpiece!"
— Rev. Nancy Eggert, Spiritual Director

Who Cares?
Simple Ways YOU Can Reach Out
Ave Maria Press, Original Publisher

Praise for *Who Cares?*:

A lonely neighbor, a colleague in distress, a friend in difficulty. In situations like these we want to reach out and help, yet so often we feel unsure about our response.

What to do?

What to say?

What is enough?

Too much?

Too little?

This practical book is designed to bring out the caring person in each of us. Marcy Heidish offers simple, specific ways to practice the art of caring, especially within our immediate circle of concern: family, friends, neighbors, and coworkers.

Heidish reminds us of the many little things we can do to open the door to a caring relationship.

— **Ave Maria Press**

Contains savvy insights and wisdom about service. This is an ideal resource for anyone interested in engaged spirituality." — ***Cultural Information Service***

Too Late To Be A Fortune Cookie Writer

A novelist has a specific poetic license which also applies to his own life.
~ Jerzi Kosinski

Marcy Heidish, award-winning author of fiction and non-fiction, is just such a novelist with a specific poetic license."
Her work has been praised for its lyrical grace" and so it is a special joy to present her first book of poetry. Ms. Heidish has written poems for decades.

With humor and humanity, this collection spans a broad range of subjects. Insight, wit and depth enliven these poems. They address universal concerns: maturity, mortality, memory and much more.

Ms. Heidish gives us an intimate glimpse into a writer's soul. Adept at varied verse forms, she amuses, reflects, recalls, and rejoices:

*"A watched pot never boils unless you're boiling vodka."
*"Houses crowd my life like chairs on a November beach."
*"The sun is a peach, half ripened, at hand."

And the poet brings us with her.

BURNING THE MAID:
POEMS FOR JOAN OF ARC

Joan was a being so uplifted from the ordinary run of mankind that she finds no equal in a thousand years.... Her story would be beyond belief if it were not true.
—Winston Churchill

She is the Wonder of the Ages. And when we consider her origin, her early circumstances, her sex, and that she did all the things upon which her renown rests while she was a young girl, we recognize that while our race continues, she will also be the Riddle of the Ages.
—Mark Twain

Here, in poetry, is a fresh approach to Joan of Arc, that famous heroine-for-all-seasons. Almost six hundred years after she was burned at the stake, Joan's story still compels, fascinates and challenges us.

Credited with saving France, that famous warrior-maid leaps from a new poetry collection by Marcy Heidish, a gifted specialist in historical fiction (*A Woman Called Moses, Destined to Dance*, etc). Heidish's poetic reflections on Joan are riveting, imaginative, and beautifully crafted.

Whether you know a little or a lot about Joan of Arc, this original and elegant collection will invite you to see "The Maid of Orleans" from a wealth of insightful perspectives. If you approach Joan as a role model, a puzzle, or a poem herself, you will find this book an impressive and inspiring read.

WHERE DO THINGS GO?

This luminous book of poems from the award-winning author goes deeper and lighter at once and speaks to the reader in an engaging manner: spirited, sassy and sensitive.

Where Do Things Go? offers fresh reflections on everyday life, expressed with humor, insight, and lyrical grace.

In a conversational tone, Ms. Heidish takes on delight, death, beauty, and the ironies of living. Rediscover yourself in this poetic mirror for today's adults, challenged by changing times.

Praise for *Who Cares?*:

Kirkus Review, featuring *Where Do Things Go?* as one of its **Books of the Month** AND **one of its Books of the Year**:

"A powerful collection of poetry in which humor is tinged with sadness, and grief is leavened with warmth.

"In her third book of poetry, Heidish (Destined to Dance, 2012, etc.) experiments with punctuation, spacing, and the physical shape of texts. Most often, she writes in free verse as she reflects on her life as writer, poet, and instructor....

"Heidish addresses more quotidian concerns, such as the impatience of a doctor's waiting room, the indignities of summer, and the nature of hats.

"She also writes in the voice of a neglected pet fish and wonders how bears receive her discarded writings as they rifle through the garbage.

"A poem about a 60th birthday celebration features 'all of those tiny candles, / studding a long barge of tiramisu,' and the speaker wryly calls for legislative action limiting the number of candles permitted by law, for the safety of us all....

"Poems full of linguistic delights and keen emotion."

A MISPLACED WOMAN
A NOVEL of Courage in Verse

"This cycle of poems explores homelessness through one woman's experience of falling from her privileged, educated background.

"Heidish, an award-winning and well-published writer of fiction, nonfiction, and poetry, found inspiration for this collection from working with homeless women. The stories are fictional, but based on a notebook she kept over her 17 years of volunteering.

"Heidish chose a well-educated, upper-middle-class narrator "to show that homeless women, narrowly stereotyped, come from all strata of society" —always true, but especially so in the current economy. This choice can make for unexpected, striking images, as when her narrator is glad for the poetry she memorized in college: "I sleep on lines of iambic pentameter, / waking to that music I thought I forgot."

"Though the subject of homelessness may sound over-earnest, Heidish's powerful voice, often bolstered by rhyme and meter, makes this collection as tough and resilient as its subjects. But the poet locates far more than toughness in her homeless women; she makes the reader see their undeniable (but too often denied, and thus tragic) humanity...."

"The images are surprising and fresh, which makes an effective counterpart to the often somber tone....

"The narrator's openness to grace gives the wrenching collection its soul...."

"A collection that beautifully finds the holy in the eccentric, the homeless, and the disregarded."

A **Kirkus Review Book of the Month AND Book of the Year**.

Short Pieces:

Articles and book reviews published in *Ms. Magazine*, *GEO* Magazine, *The Washington Post*, *The Washington Star*, and various in-flight periodicals.

Two of these pieces are:

● *The Pilgrim Who Stayed*, **GEO Magazine**, about Chartres Cathedral, widely translated.

● *The Grand Dame of the Harbor*, about the Statue of Liberty, was a highly acclaimed cover story for **GEO Magazine**. This article is included in a textbook anthology designed to teach writing to college students. Winner of coveted Apex Award.

See Marcy Heidish page at:

www.Amazon.com **[AND Kindle] ***

www.marcyheidishbooks.com

Marcy Heidish Books are printed by Lightning Source and distributed by Ingram of Ingram Content Group Inc., the world's largest distributor of physical and digital content, providing books, music and media content to over 38,000 retailers, libraries, schools and distribution partners in 195 countries. More than 25,000 publishers use Ingram's.

INDEX